ALIENS InVaded My Talent Show!

TO SAM AND JOE,
YOU TWO ARE
THE BEST

First published in the UK in 2018 by Usborne Publishing Ltd., Usborne House,
83-85 Saffron Hill, London EC1N 8RT, England. www.usborne.com

Text copyright © Matt Brown, 2018
Illustrations by Paco Sordo © Usborne Publishing Ltd., 2018

A CIP catalogue record for this book is available from the British Library.

ISBN 9781474933667 04436/1 JFMA JJASOND/18
Printed in the UK.

BY **Matt Brown**

ALIENS Invaded My Talent Show!

ILLUSTRATED BY **PACO SORDO**

USBORNE

FRIDAY

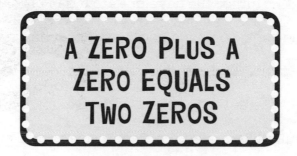

A ZERO PLUS A ZERO EQUALS TWO ZEROS

In the whole of his entire, actual life, Eric Doomsday had never got anything through the post.

No letters, no postcards, no parcels, no nothing.

He did get a pizza menu once, although, as it had been addressed to a Mrs Eric Dumsday, he didn't think it counted.

And yet here he was, standing in his bedroom, holding a purple envelope that had just been delivered to *his* house, that had *his* name written on it. Eric turned the envelope around in his hands. On the back, someone had drawn beautiful swirls and spirals in silver ink, and it had been sealed with a large red star. Hands trembling, Eric carefully lifted open the flap. Inside was a small piece of golden paper. It was an invitation.

Eric held his breath and looked again at the front of the envelope, just to make doubly sure that he hadn't accidentally opened something that was addressed to someone else. He had made that mistake once before with a letter that he thought had been for him but that had, in fact, been addressed to his Auntie Elsie. She had been staying with them while her house was being redecorated. Before Eric realized his mistake, he had spent a very worrying twenty minutes thinking he needed to get a rather large boil removed from his bottom.

But this time there was no mistake.

He, Eric Doomsday, of number 18 Ottershaw Drive, had been invited to a birthday party. And not just any birthday party either. No, Eric had been invited to *Hattie Lavernock's* birthday party. He stood there, in his vest, pants and socks, staring at the golden invitation, and lost himself in a daydream of party games and laughter.

DING DONG DING DONG DING DONG

Eric's daydream was shattered by the sound of someone ringing the front doorbell, followed, a few moments later, by the thunder of heavy footsteps coming up the stairs, and a barrage of excited squeals.

"OHMYGOSHOHMYGOSHOHMYGOSH!"

Eric's best friend, Vinnie Mumbles, crashed through his bedroom door, a huge smile plastered right across her face. In fact, Vinnie was so excited that her brain seemed to completely ignore that she was standing in front of a boy in his vest and pants.

"I got one too," said Eric, holding up his invitation. In his state of extreme excitement, his brain had also seemed to completely ignore that he was standing in front of a girl in his vest and pants.

Vinnie grabbed it from his still trembling hand and walked over to the window. She held them up to the light, like she was checking to see if they were forgeries.

"It...it's real," she said, beaming. "It's only blummin' real."

8

The excitement of getting an invitation to Hattie Lavernock's birthday party suddenly burst out of Eric in all directions and he did a little happy dance. Unfortunately, as he did, his foot slipped on some playing cards that lay strewn on the carpet and he fell backwards into a half-eaten bowl of cornflakes that he'd put on his chair for safekeeping.

Vinnie clasped the invitations to her chest.

"This is our chance," she said.

Eric stood up from the chair and tried to reach the bowl that was now, thanks to the soggy cereal, glued onto his left bottom cheek. He let out a small sigh. He was sick and tired of accidentally getting things stuck onto different bits of his body. Last week, Eric had somehow managed to get the bread bin jammed on his foot while he had been making some toast. And then only yesterday, the World Marble Championship Final that Eric was playing against himself in his bedroom had to be interrupted when he got the waste-paper bin stuck on his head.

"Chance for what?" he said.

Vinnie smiled. "Our chance to be liked," she

said, watching Eric waggle his bum around. "How many parties have you ever been to before?"

Eric stopped waggling.

"Er..." he said.

"That weren't your own," added Vinnie.

"Er..." said Eric, still thinking.

"Or mine," added Vinnie.

"Er..." said Eric again.

"Or your grandma's," said Vinnie.

Eric counted on his fingers.

"Er, well, none," he said.

"Exactly," said Vinnie. "It's the same with me. Our class has thirty pupils in it so, since we started school, there have been a grand total of 168 birthdays and we haven't been invited to any. On a popularity scale of one to ten, we are a pair of zeros."

"So why has Hattie Lavernock invited us this year?" said Eric. "She must be at least a ten."

"Search me," said Vinnie. "Hey, maybe she got a kick out of the last presentation I did to the class? You know, the one on the history of the internal combustion engine that Ms Mustering gave me top marks for."

Vinnie gave Eric their special secret smile where she curled her fingers around her top lip like a moustache and opened her eyes as wide as they would go.

But Eric didn't have a chance to

say what he thought of Vinnie's theory because, at that moment, with a loud slurping noise, the cereal bowl unstuck itself from his left bottom cheek and slithered and slopped down his leg. It left behind a large trail of soggy cornflakes that made it look like Eric had had a terrible accident before he could get to the toilet.

SATURDAY

HATTIE LAVERNOCK'S BIRTHDAY PARTY

"What on **EARTH** are you two doing here?"

Hattie Lavernock held open her front door and stared at Eric and Vinnie. Eric could feel his whole face going red.

"Well, I invited them, dear," said Hattie's mum, appearing behind Hattie in the doorway. "It's your last birthday at primary school so I invited everyone from your class. I thought it would be nice."

"B-b-but..." said Hattie, a look of astonished fury in her eyes. She simply couldn't believe that the two least popular people in the whole class had been invited to her party.

Vinnie ran a hand nervously down the skirt of her red dress.

"Come in, come in," said Mrs Lavernock, waving Eric and Vinnie inside the house. "You've arrived just in time."

They walked through the doorway and into the Lavernocks' hall. All the while, Hattie stared at them so hard that Eric thought her eyes might pop out of her head. Grace Smeaton and Drishya Samode appeared behind Hattie. Grace looked Vinnie up and down and whispered something to Drishya. They both sniggered and Vinnie looked away. Hattie gave one last withering look at Eric and Vinnie before snorting like a disgusted pig and stomping off (also like a disgusted pig). Grace and Drishya followed her.

"Well, come through to the sitting room," said Mrs Lavernock, seemingly oblivious to the awkwardness. "The party has just started. We're about to give Hattie her main present."

In the living room, everyone from their class was standing in a semicircle around Hattie's father, who was holding a large dome-shaped present wrapped up in beautiful purple-and-gold paper.

"Happy birthday, Hattie," he said.

Hattie rushed over and ripped off the wrapping paper.

"Oh, Mummy, oh, Daddy, it's what I've always wanted," she said, gazing at a small green bird inside a large golden cage.

"It's a parrot," said Mr Lavernock. "And we've already trained it to say something, just for you."

"Actually," whispered Vinnie to Eric, "it's called a Quaker parrot, which is sometimes known as a monk parakeet. You can tell by the markings."

"Oh," said Eric.

"It's native to subtropical South American countries and is the only parrot to build a stick nest," said Vinnie.

"Oh," said Eric again, not surprised in the least by Vinnie's expert parrot knowledge. In his experience, she knew just about everything.

Mr Lavernock flipped the latch on the cage

door and opened it.
The parrot flew
out and circled
around the
Lavernocks' living
room before landing
on the ceiling lampshade.

But, as Hattie squealed with delight, Mrs Lavernock's phone beeped with some bad news. As a special birthday treat, Hattie's mum and dad had booked **The Amazing Alan**, Dreary Inkling's greatest living party magician, to come and perform. Unfortunately, he had just texted to say that he was currently stuck inside a suit of armour, which had been wrapped up in chains and padlocks, and then put inside a large sack, which had also been wrapped up in chains and padlocks, and then put inside a large wooden box, which had also been wrapped up in chains and padlocks, and then put inside a wardrobe, which had also been wrapped up in chains and padlocks, before finally being dropped into a large shark-filled tank of water, which had also been wrapped up in chains and padlocks. The Amazing Alan had forgotten the combination number of the first padlock and thought he would probably be stuck for some time.

Hattie Lavernock burst into tears.

"Oh, don't cry, Hattiekins," said Mrs Lavernock, fussing around her. "Not on your birthday."

Eric turned and saw that Vinnie was staring at him. A smile slowly spread across her face.

"Eric can do magic tricks," she said. "He's very good at them."

Everyone turned and looked at Eric, who went bright red again.

"What are you doing?" he hissed at Vinnie.

"Impress this lot with some of your amazing tricks and they might like us," she whispered. "We might finally become popular."

Hattie looked at Eric suspiciously.

"Can you really do magic?" she sniffed. "I didn't think you could do anything."

The truth was, Eric couldn't just *do* magic, he *loved* magic. He'd been obsessed with card tricks and illusions since his seventh birthday. He spent most of his spare time practising special card shuffles and making things look like they were vanishing from his hands. It's just that when it came to showing off his skills, he got embarrassed and shy.

"Would you do some tricks, Eric?" said Mrs Lavernock. "You'd totally be saving the day."

Eric looked around nervously at the faces of all his classmates as they stared at him, and then at Vinnie, who smiled and gave him a big thumbs up.

"Erm...er...okay," he said.

Mrs Lavernock clapped her hands in excitement.

"Oh, Eric," she said, "that's so kind of you. You're an absolute hero. I tell you what, you do some magic and I'll go and get the cake."

She didn't know it at the time, but they would be the very last words that Mrs Lavernock ever spoke to Eric Doomsday.

ERIC DoOMSDAY'S TRAIL oF DESTRUCTION

Eric slipped his deck of cards out of their box and smiled. He took them everywhere, and he loved everything about them. The way they smelled, the sound they made as he riffle-shuffled them, how they flowed like water when he fanned them out...

He began his routine by pulling a card out of thin air and then making it vanish again. Hattie Lavernock made a face like she was sort of impressed but didn't want to show it. Next, Eric got Ernie Splott to blindfold him, select a card from the pack, put it back in the middle of the deck and give the cards a good shuffle. With a click of his fingers, Eric made the card vanish from the deck and reappear in Ernie's back pocket. Hattie gasped and clapped when she saw that one. And when she started clapping, so did everyone else – even when Eric forgot to take his blindfold off and fell over Mrs Lavernock's magazine rack. Eric beamed. He couldn't believe it was going so well.

Next, Eric did a trick where he made a glass magically teleport through the table, before bringing his routine to a spectacular close by bending a regular spoon using only the power of

his mind. And as Eric performed his miracles, Hattie and the party crowd *ooooooh*hed and *aahhhhhh*hed and clapped. After the final cheers and applause had died down, Mrs Lavernock wheeled in a large trolley.

"Okay, here comes the cake," she said. "There's chocolate cake on the bottom, Victoria sponge on top of that, lemon cake on top of that, peanut-butter marble cake on top of that and ice-cream cake at the very top."

Mrs Lavernock pushed the trolley around the room, unable to contain her pride at the cake that

she had spent the last three days constructing. "Happy birthday, Hattie," she said. "As Eric performed such wonderful magic, why don't you give him the first slice?"

Hattie nodded and smiled and began to cut the cake.

"Squawk! Happy birthday, Hattie! Squawk!" said the parrot.

Eric had never, ever felt more popular than he did at that moment. He had to be at least a six or a seven on the popularity chart now, and he wanted that feeling to go on for ever. So he decided that he would do another trick, just for Hattie.

He took a coin from his pocket and began to perform the classic "pulling a coin out of someone's ear" trick. It was an easy illusion that Eric had practised in his room hundreds of times. Everything was going brilliantly until Eric ended the trick by pulling the coin out of Hattie's ear with what magicians call a "flourish". A "flourish" is an extreme or extravagant arm movement which magicians do to make them look more mysterious and magic-y. Unfortunately, Eric *over-flourished* – throwing his hand back with such force that it smashed into the five-tiered, multicoloured cake that was sitting on the trolley just behind him.

His hand crashed into the top, ice-cream layer of the cake, karate-chopping it slap-bang into Mrs Lavernock's face. Blinded by delicious ice cream, Mrs Lavernock stumbled around in shock for a moment, only to trip forwards into the cake trolley, flipping it up into the air and sending the rest of the cake flying across the room.

The next twenty seconds seemed to happen in slow motion. Eric could only watch in horror as the cake broke apart in mid-air and covered the whole of the Lavernocks' living room in a gooey multicoloured mess. The floral settee was splattered with shards of chocolate cake, and the massive sixty-four-inch wall-mounted surround-sound TV took a direct hit from a huge piece of peanut-butter marble cake. Everyone in the room was showered with sponge and whipped cream and icing. Eric himself took a large chunk of lemon cake right in the face and Vinnie got sprayed with hundreds and thousands. Some people were screaming in terror as they ran for cover, others were laughing hysterically as they grabbed great fistfuls of cake and hurled it across the room, adding to the carnage.

And above all the chaos, Mrs Lavernock could be heard shouting things like "MY PARQUET FLOORING!" and "PLEASE, NOT THE FAMILY PORTRAIT!" and "WHY ME? FOR THE LOVE OF ALL THAT IS GOOD IN THE WORLD, WHY???" And every time she yelled something the green parrot squawked it right back at her.

In the middle of it all, Eric saw Grace and Drishya howling and crying as Hattie slipped and slithered in a large pile of chocolate cake and ice cream. Her brand-new pretty party dress and her special braided hairdo were completely covered in sticky, brown gloop.

"Hattie!" screeched Mrs Lavernock.

"Squawk! Hattie, Hattie! Squawk!" repeated the parrot, as it flew down from the lampshade and landed on Hattie Lavernock's head, before doing a huge poo all down her face.

Hattie Lavernock let out a wail of despair. "WWWWAAAAAAAAHHHHHHHHH!"

Seeing her daughter covered in cake gunk and bird plops caused Hattie Lavernock's mum to shout out the third-worst swear word in the world, which the parrot then repeated over and over and over and over and over.

From where he stood, dazed and confused and covered in cake, Eric assumed that his trail of destruction was as bad as life could get. But he was wrong. Because life was about to get a whole lot worse for Eric Doomsday.

SUNDAY

NEARLY THREE
BILLION MILES AWAY

A gleaming interstellar SpaceCruiser 689908, with

the words *GALAXY INSPECTORS* written on the

side, slowed out of hyper speed and parked itself

just to the left-hand side of Neptune.

"We have arrived, Your Mightiness. The next life forms for inspection inhabit one of the eight planets in this solar system."

"SO WHICH ONE ARE WE GOING TO? THE ONE WITH THE RINGS? THAT LOOKS QUITE NICE. OR THE ONE WITH THE BIG RED SPOT? I BET THAT'S LOVELY."

"No, Your Mightiness. We will be going to the third one from the star. The blue and green planet."

"REALLY? IT LOOKS VERY SMALL. WHAT'S IT CALLED?"

"The directory says that the inhabitants refer to it as the planet 'Earth'."

A gigantic screen flashed up an image of the planet Earth.

"THE PLANET UUURRTH?"

"That's right, Your Mightiness. The planet Earth."

"URRRRTH. UUUUURRRRTHH. HOW DISGUSTING. IT SOUNDS LIKE THE SORT OF NOISE YOU'D MAKE IF YOU WERE BEING SICK."

"Yes, Your Mightiness."

"SO, WHO WILL WE BE INSPECTING THEN?"

"The life forms are called humans, Your Mightiness."

"HMMMM. 'HUMANS-YOUR-MIGHTINESS'. THAT'S A BIT OF A FUNNY NAME, ISN'T IT?"

"Er, no, Your Mightiness, the life forms are not called 'humans-your-mightiness'. They are just called 'humans'. Your Mightiness."

"THAT'S EXACTLY WHAT I JUST SAID,

'HUMANS-YOUR-MIGHTINESS'."

"Forgive me, Your Mightiness, but if they were called 'humans-your-mightiness' then I would have called them 'humans-your-mightiness', Your Mightiness."

"ARE YOU TRYING TO BE FUNNY?"

"No, Your Mightiness."

"BECAUSE I DON'T LIKE IT WHEN OTHER LIFE FORMS TRY TO BE FUNNY."

"No, Your Mightiness."

"I TEND TO VAPORIZE OTHER LIFE FORMS WHO TRY TO BE FUNNY."

"Yes, Your Mightiness."

"WHICH, AS IT TURNS OUT, IS ACTUALLY VERY FUNNY."

"Yes, Your Mightiness."

"SO, HAS A LOCATION BEEN CHOSEN FOR OUR INSPECTION?"

"The directory has selected the perfect inspection zone, Your Mightiness. It is a small area known as Dreary Inkling and it is full of the human life forms."

"GOOD. NOW LET US JUST HOPE THAT THEY PASS THE INSPECTION."

"Yes, Your Mightiness."

"BECAUSE WE ARE SUPPOSED TO BE GOING ON HOLIDAY AFTER WE'VE BEEN TO UUURRTH."

"Yes, Your Mightiness."

"AND IF THEY FAIL THE INSPECTION AND WE HAVE TO VAPORIZE THE PLANET, IT WILL START EATING INTO OUR BEACH TIME."

"Yes, Your Mightiness."

"WHICH REMINDS ME. DID YOU PACK MY TRUNKS?"

"Yes, Your Mightiness."

"GOOD, GOOD. MY NICE RED ONES WITH YELLOW SPOTS?"

"Yes, Your Mightiness."

"EXCELLENT. SO, DO WE HAVE ANY IDEA WHAT THESE HUMANS LOOK LIKE?"

The image on the screen changed from the picture of the Earth to show a man of about forty-two or forty-three years old, wearing a T-shirt and trousers and scratching his bottom.

"OH DEAR."

"Oh dear, Your Mightiness."

"OH DEAR, OH DEAR, OH DEAR. THEY

DON'T LOOK VERY PROMISING, DO THEY?"

"No, they don't, Your Mightiness."

"TELL YOU WHAT, LET'S GET THE PLANET-VAPORIZING RAY WARMED UP, JUST IN CASE THEY FAIL THE INSPECTION."

"Yes, Your Mightiness."

"BECAUSE FROM THE LOOK OF THEM, THEY PROBABLY WILL."

"Yes, Your Mightiness."

"OKAY, LET'S GO. IS THE CLOAKING DEVICE WORKING NOW? BECAUSE WE DON'T WANT

ANY OF THESE HUMANS TO SEE OUR SPACECRUISER."

"The cloaking device is fully operational, Your Mightiness."

"GOOD."

"Well, almost."

"ALMOST?"

"Yes, it has been flicking on and off recently, but it's hardly doing it at all at the moment."

"WELL, THESE HUMANS DON'T LOOK LIKE THE MOST OBSERVANT OF SPECIES, DO THEY?"

"No, Your Mightiness."

"THEY LOOK A BIT STUPID, TO BE HONEST."

"Yes, Your Mightiness. I'm quite sure it won't be a problem."

"ALRIGHT THEN, ACTIVATE THE ALMOST FULLY OPERATIONAL CLOAKING DEVICE."

"Activating cloaking device now, Your Mightiness."

"AND ALSO ACTIVATE SOME SNACKS FOR THE JOURNEY."

"Yes, Your Mightiness."

And with that, the huge, gleaming interstellar SpaceCruiser 689908 that was parked just to the left-hand side of Neptune disappeared.

Then it reappeared and began to move towards Earth.

Then it disappeared again.

OVER

The Dreary Inkling night sky was dark and clear and the stars sparkled like scattered diamonds on a velvet cloth.

"I don't see it." Eric peered through his telescope. "Actually, Vinnie, I don't see much of anything. Over."

The small plastic walkie-talkie he was holding hissed for a moment and then a voice crackled out.

"Are you looking in the right place? Try moving the telescope around a bit. Over."

Eric made a large figure-of-eight motion with the telescope.

"Nope," he said, clicking the button on the side of the walkie-talkie. "Nothing. Over."

The walkie-talkie crackled.

"Try adjusting the focus. Use the knob by the eyepiece. But hurry, the meteor shower is supposed to happen any minute. It's going to be awesome. Over."

"Well, I wouldn't know about that because my telescope isn't working," muttered Eric, twiddling the focus knob.

The walkie-talkie crackled again.

"Have you taken the lens cap off? Over."

Eric snorted.

"Of course I've taken the lens cap off," he mumbled to himself. "Honestly, I'm not a total—"

Eric stopped as he looked along the barrel of the telescope and saw that he hadn't, in fact, taken the lens cap off. He quickly pulled it away from the front of the telescope and stuffed it in his pocket. He clicked the button on the side of the walkie-talkie.

"Er, I think I've fixed the problem," he said.

Despite being two houses away from Vinnie, Eric could feel her rolling her eyes at him.

He took a breath. "Right, where do I need to look? Over."

"*Find the North Star*," said Vinnie. "*Then elevate three degrees. Over.*"

Eric squinted through the eyepiece. "I can see three bright stars all close together in a line. Is one of those the North Star? Over."

The walkie-talkie hissed.

"*That's Orion's belt,*" said Vinnie. "*You're way off. You need to—*" There was a pause and then: "*I can see them, I can see them!*" she shrieked. "*They're beautiful. Like fireworks. Quick, Eric, you need to go left. Over.*"

Eric moved his telescope to the left.

"Wait," he said, adjusting the focus. "I think I've got it. I can see one right now. Over."

"Brilliant, isn't it?" said Vinnie. "How many can you see? Over."

Eric twiddled the focus knob again.

"Only one," he said. "But it's really bright and it's flashing red and gold. Do they always do that? Over."

There was a pause and the static from the walkie-talkie spluttered quietly. Then it crackled back into life.

"Repeat," said Vinnie. "Over."

"I was just wondering if all meteors flashed red and gold," said Eric. "I assumed they'd be sort of white."

The walkie-talkie hissed.

"Er, over," he added.

The walkie-talkie crackled again.

"*What are you talking about? Over*," said Vinnie.

"Oh wait," said Eric. "It's getting bigger. Do meteors do that? Do they get bigger? Over."

"*What? Wait, where exactly are you looking? Over.*"

"Just to the left of, er, thingy's belt," said Eric. "You know, O'Brian, or whatever he was called. Oh no, wait..."

"*What?*" said Vinnie.

"It's gone," said Eric. "There was just this kind of purple streak in the sky, like a flash of lightning, and then it just...well, it just vanished. Didn't you see it? Over."

"No," said Vinnie. "I don't know what you were looking at but it definitely wasn't a meteor. It was probably an aeroplane or something like that. Over."

But despite being both a team leader at the Dreary Inkling Astronomical Society (DrInkASOc) and the founding member of the Year Six lunchtime science club, Vinnie Mumbles was wrong. The light that Eric saw wasn't an aeroplane. It was a gleaming interstellar SpaceCruiser 689908 with a temperamental cloaking device, that had just travelled nearly three billion miles across the solar system. And inside the ship was an alien species that had the power to destroy the entire planet, and who had also just run out of snacks and was pretty cross about it.

RED EYE

Eric opened his eyes and looked at the clock on his bedside table.

It said 11.47 p.m.

A noise coming from the back garden had woken him up a few minutes ago. A scraping, scratching, scrabbling sort of sound.

At first he had thought it was the sound of his mum and dad snoring, and so he had tried to get back to the dream he'd been having about creating a ROBOCALYPSE where his army of giant robots took over the world. But then he'd heard the noise again and it had definitely been coming from outside.

He sat up in bed and made a small gap in his curtains. Some clouds had gathered, covering the moon, and the back garden was shrouded in darkness.

Eric heard the noise for a third time. The scratching and scraping sounded like it was coming from behind the garden shed, over by the fence.

"Probably a fox," he mumbled, wiping the sleep from the corner of his eye.

Sitting as still as he could, Eric peered into the gloom. Suddenly, he saw a large shadow move out into the garden from behind the shed. A large shadow that had two red eyes which burned in the darkness. Eric wanted to turn away but he couldn't. His whole body was stuck, rooted to the spot. He watched as the red eyes began to move towards the house. Eric's breathing got faster and faster and his heart was thumping so hard he thought it might burst out of his chest. The shadow came closer and closer and closer until...

BLAM!

The Doomsdays' anti-burglar light clicked on and flooded the garden with light. Eric gasped, expecting to see whatever the red eyes belonged to. But there was nothing.

No shadow.

No red eyes.

Just garden.

Eric breathed a big sigh of relief.

"You've got to stop eating cheese before bed," he muttered to himself and yawned a big yawn.

The anti-intruder light clicked off and Eric went back to sleep.

But as he snored and dreamed, something did move in the garden below. Something big and unearthly with two red eyes that burned like embers from the fires of hell.

MONDAY

MINTON

When Eric woke up the next morning he checked outside his bedroom window. To his great relief, the back garden was quiet and there wasn't any sign of anything weird or shadowy or red-eyed. So he put on his school uniform and headed downstairs for breakfast.

His dad was striding around the kitchen with his hands on his hips, shouting into a small microphone that came out of his ear.

"C'mon, Geoff, I know it's only 7.52 a.m. here but it's nearly 4 p.m. in Tokyo!"

Eric walked over to the cupboard to get some cereal but his dad was standing right in his way.

"Now, Geoff, I want you to make my eight o'clock an 8.27 and turn my two o'clock into a four o'clock," he said. "And make the lunch thing into a brunch thing and then back into a lunch thing. And then—"

Eric's dad cut the sentence short. "Er, hang on, Geoff, there's another call coming in on the other line."

Mr Doomsday pushed a button on his mobile phone to switch lines.

"Hello, You've Been Drained, Si Doomsday here?"

"Hi, Dad," said Eric, speaking into the house phone just behind his father. "Can you pass me the cornflakes, please?"

Mr Doomsday reached into the cupboard that he was standing in front of, took out the packet of cornflakes and handed it to Eric.

"That's an affirmative, son," he said. "I'd love to know how successfully the cereal performs. Can you give me some feedback in the next twenty-four hours?"

Without waiting for a reply, Eric's dad pushed a button on his mobile phone to switch lines back to Geoff again. Mr Doomsday was always unbelievably busy and made hundreds of phone calls every day. He had just started his own business, called You've Been Drained, which helped people unblock their drains.

Eric took his cornflakes to the table and ate them while his dad continued to shout down the phone at Geoff about sewage. As Eric finished his last mouthful, he heard his mum yelling in the garden. He went outside to investigate and found her standing by the fence near the back of the garden shed, telling off their dog.

"Minton! Look what you've done to the fence!" Eric's mum was pointing at two large arcs of deep claw marks. "My lovely new fence," she said. "It's completely ruined, you naughty dog."

Minton wandered back into the house and came out a few seconds later with something black flapping in his mouth. Eric and his mum were both still busy looking at the claw marks on the fence. Eric was just thinking how much bigger than Minton's paws they looked when he heard the gate click and saw Vinnie walking up the path.

"Morning, Lavinia," said Eric's mum.

"Morning," said Vinnie. "Hey, what happened to your fence?"

"Minton has been a bad dog," said Mrs Doomsday.

Vinnie looked at the claw marks. "They're quite big," she said.

Eric was just about to agree with her when his mum started shouting again and rushed off after the dog.

"Minton! No!"

For a moment, Eric and Vinnie watched as Eric's mum wrestled with Minton in the mud.

"Naughty, naughty dog!" she shouted, as she pulled one of her best black frilly bras from a half-dug hole by the rosebush. "Bad Minton!"

Vinnie looked at Eric. "There's no way Minton made those marks," she said.

Eric nodded. "They're too big, aren't they?" he said. And, remembering the strange noises he had heard in the garden, a terrifying thought struck him. "But if he didn't make them, then what did?"

BoTTOM PLoPPAGE SCooPAGE

The control panel of the interstellar SpaceCruiser 689908 blinked and flashed, as the spaceship hovered silently and invisibly three hundred miles above Dreary Inkling. Two pairs of red eyes watched a large screen that showed what was happening in the village down below.

"SO, OUR INSPECTION OF THE PLANET UURRTH HAS BEGUN. WHAT DID YOU FIND?"

"Well, Your Mightiness, I began my inspection

in the area marked red on the map, known locally as Ottershaw Drive."

"SOUNDS REVOLTING."

"It is mainly an area of human dwellings, Your Mightiness. Nothing of interest to report, so I travelled to the area marked in yellow, known locally as the High Street."

"UGH! I HATE IT ALREADY."

"It was here that I observed one human dragging another, smaller Earth animal around on some sort of lead that was tied around its neck."

"WHAT? HOW WEIRD."

"Yes, Your Mightiness, but that is not all. The smaller animal stopped and did an enormous great expulsion of ploppage from its bottom parts, right on the pavement."

"BOTTOM PLOPPAGE? ON THE PAVEMENT? HOW DISGUSTING."

"Yes, Your Mightiness, but that's not all. The human then patted the smaller Earth animal on the head and said 'Who's a good boy, then?' It was as if the human was pleased about the bottom ploppage."

"REVOLTING!"

"Yes, Your Mightiness, but that's not all. The human then scooped up the bottom ploppage in a small bag and carried it away."

"BOTTOM PLOPPAGE SCOOPAGE? UTTERLY SICKENING! SOMETIMES BEING A GALAXY INSPECTOR CAN BE A HORRIBLE JOB."

"Absolutely, Your Mightiness."

The two pairs of eyes looked again at the screen.

"WHAT'S HAPPENING OVER THERE?" A long sharp talon tapped on the bit of the screen that was showing Dreary Inkling Primary School. "WHAT ARE ALL THOSE SHORT HUMANS DOING GOING INTO THAT BUILDING?"

"It's some kind of learning facility, Your Mightiness. It's where they train their young."

One set of red eyes narrowed.

"GOOD, WE DEFINITELY NEED TO INSPECT THAT."

"Very good, Your Mightiness."

His Mightiness dropped onto all fours, muscles bunching in his powerful hindquarters as he prowled over to the control panel. All the while, his red eyes smouldered at the screen.

"JUST LOOK AT THEIR PUNY BOTTOM LIMBS AND TINY HEADS. THEY ARE SO UGLY. YOU CAN'T EVEN SEE THEIR BRAINS. WE COULD CRUSH THEM IN A SECOND."

"Certainly, Your Mightiness, although Section 1878 of the Intergalactic Convention does frown on head-crushing before an inspection has been completed."

"YES, YES, YOU ARE RIGHT. WE MUST INSPECT THEM FIRST TO SEE IF THEY ARE WORTHY OF LIFE BEFORE WE VAPORIZE THEM. AND YOU NEVER KNOW, THESE HUMANS MIGHT PASS THE INSPECTION AND THEN WE WON'T HAVE TO DESTROY THEM AFTER ALL."

The red eyes looked at each other, then both Galaxy Inspectors burst out laughing.

"HA HA HA HA HA HA HA."

"Ha ha ha ha ha ha ha. Good one, Your Mightiness."

"RIGHT THEN, SHALL WE RESUME OUR INSPECTION?"

"Well, Your Mightiness, we need to disguise ourselves before teleporting down to the planet."

"OH GOOD, I LOVE DISGUISES. WHAT ARE WE DOING THIS TIME?"

"The directory has found an Earth book all about local fashions. It is using it now to create a series of outfits for us to wear. We will blend in perfectly."

"EXCELLENT, WHAT'S THE BOOK CALLED?"

"It's called *The 1980s, the Time that Fashion Forgot.*"

"GOOD, THEN LET US BEGIN. THERE IS MUCH WORK TO BE DONE."

DANK
GRIM HOOT

Eric trudged through the school gates, his hands buried in his trouser pockets, looking like he had all the trouble of the world stacked on his shoulders. Ever since what had happened at Hattie Lavernock's birthday party, he had been dreading coming to school and facing people. Vinnie glanced up from the book she was reading and saw the look on Eric's face.

"Eric, you need to stop worrying," she said.

"Everyone has probably forgotten all about it."

Eric looked at her. He was not convinced.

As they walked into the school playground, Eric glanced up at the sign that greeted visitors. There had been a time when it had said:

WELCOME TO DREARY INKLING PRIMARY

SCHOOL EST. 1991

But because so many of the letters and numbers had fallen off and nobody had bothered to replace them, it now said:

WELCOME TO D A. NK G RIM.

HOO T.

They crossed the faded hopscotch grid and past Max Frameraté and Johnny Smuthers from Year Four. When they saw Eric, they rushed over.

"Is it true?" said Max Frameraté, trying to catch his breath. "That you caused a cake fight at Hattie's party?"

"Er, well, er, I," stammered Eric.

"And that you made her parrot do a massive poo all over her face?" said Johnny Smuthers.

"Er, well, er, I," stammered Eric again.

"And that you made her mum say the third worst swear word in the world?" said Max Frameraté.

"Er...well...er...I..." said Eric, who could feel himself going red.

"Amazing!" they shrieked, and ran off howling with laughter.

Eric turned to Vinnie. "So everyone's forgotten about it?" he said.

"Well, look on the bright side," said Vinnie, as the bell rang for the start of school. "Not everyone thinks you're a loser."

Eric sighed. "I feel awful about what happened," he said. "I am never doing magic tricks again." He shoved his hands in his pockets as he walked towards the main entrance. But as he did, his foot somehow managed to get caught in one of the playground potholes.

He stumbled and fought to keep his balance, his arms whirling around like he was a crazed double-windmill. And before he knew what was happening, Eric had crashed into someone, sending them both clattering to the floor in a heap. Someone who looked an awful lot like Hattie Lavernock.

A group of Year Two kids, who had seen everything, screeched with laughter as Eric staggered to his feet. He dusted himself off and tried to help Hattie up. He hadn't spoken to her since what had happened at her birthday party.

"Hattie, I'm so sorry," he said. "My, er, my foot got stu—"

But before Eric had a chance to finish his sentence, Hattie Lavernock dissolved into floods of tears and ran into the school, sobbing.

The group of Year Two kids burst out laughing again.

"If it makes you feel any better," said Vinnie, putting her book into her rucksack, "in a few billion years the sun's going to explode and destroy everything in the solar system, so none of this really matters at all, does it?"

DRIPSFEST

Eric still felt terrible as he and Vinnie walked into the school hall for assembly. On the stage, their head teacher, Mrs Tittering, was attempting to flatten down a particularly unruly bit of her hair. She yawned, then picked off some dried egg from her jumper, then yawned again.

"She looks dreadful," whispered Vinnie, taking a seat on the bench at the back of the hall. "Like she's been up all night."

The reason that Mrs Tittering looked like she'd been up all night was because Mrs Tittering *had* been up all night. And the reason Mrs Tittering had been up all night was because of an email she had received the day before. It was an email from the education department of the local council and it had struck terror into Mrs Tittering's heart.

From: Lotte, Priscilla < lotte.priscilla@ thecouncil>

To: Tittering, Elvira <headteacher@drearyschool1>

Subject: ONE LAST CHANCE!

Dear Mrs Tittering,

I am writing to inform you that after our last

inspection of Dreary Inkling Primary School
we feel that certain actions must be taken.

A good school should be a place where
creativity, learning and athletic achievements
of students are encouraged and celebrated.
A place where all students, regardless of ability,
are given a platform to shine. But under your
leadership, Dreary Inkling Primary School is
failing in all these areas. It is run-down and you
seemingly have no idea how to turn this school
around.

However, we wanted to give you one last
chance to demonstrate to the education
department that your school is capable of
nurturing and developing the talents of your
pupils. An inspection team will come to your

school on Wednesday and if they don't like what they see then we will be forced to close the school down.

Yours sincerely,

Ms P.A. Lotte

After receiving the email, Mrs Tittering had spent the whole of the rest of the afternoon, and then the evening, and then the night, and then the early morning, desperately trying to think of something that would impress the inspectors and save the school. This was her first head teacher job and it was a lot harder than she'd thought it would be. She had imagined that being the head of a school meant that she could sit in a comfy chair in a warm office, drinking tea all day, and telling other people what to do. But it was not like that at all. In fact, when she tried to do any of those things, people started getting cross with her and almost never did what she asked anyway. And now this email had come and if she didn't do something she would be out of a job and Dreary Inkling would be out of a school.

But then, just after breakfast that morning, as she was sitting on her downstairs toilet, a brilliant idea hit Mrs Tittering right in the brain. The idea consisted of nine letters.

D-R-I-P-S-F-E-S-T

And as she stood onstage that Monday morning, looking out at all her pupils, those nine letters sparkled in her mind like nine shimmering stars.

"I have decided," she boomed, "that our school should have a way of—" She paused and looked at the email from the council. "Er, nurturing and developing the talents of your pupils...er, I mean, our pupils...er, I mean you."

Mrs Tittering mopped her brow.

"So, this Wednesday we are going to hold the first **DR**eary **I**nkling **P**rimary **S**chool **FEST**ival, aka **DRIPSFEST**."

A gasp went up around the school hall.

"The festival will be" – she looked at the email again – "er, a celebration of creativity, learning and athletic achievement. There's going to be a huge display of all the best artwork from all the classes in the dining hall. Throughout the festival there'll be competitions in music and mathematics

81

and dancing and poetry, and on the sports field will be the DRIPSFEST Olympics."

Whispers of excitement fluttered on the air.

"And the whole festival will begin," she continued, "with a Year Six talent show assembly, which will have a panel of judges just like on the telly."

Excited chatter broke out among the pupils.

"A talent show?" whispered Eric, beads of sweat forming on his forehead. "In two days' time?"

"Don't worry," said Vinnie. "I'm sure you won't have to do it if you don't want to."

But Mrs Tittering hadn't finished.

"And because DRIPSFEST is about, er..." She looked back at the email. "Er...giving all students a platform to shine" – she paused and scratched her cheek – "then EVERYBODY in Year Six will take part, with absolutely no exceptions."

Vinnie looked at Eric. "Are you okay?" she asked. "You've gone a bit green."

The thought of having to perform again after what had happened at Hattie Lavernock's birthday party had sent a horrible, cold, prickly sensation shooting around Eric's body.

"I-I-I..." he stammered.

Vinnie gave him their special secret smile, just

to make him feel a bit better. "Well, it could be worse," she said. "I mean, they could film it and stream it on the internet for the whole world to watch."

But Mrs Tittering still hadn't finished.

"And," she continued, "our ITC teacher, Mr Flange, has come up with the amazing idea of downloading an app on his phone so that we can stream the whole of the DRIPSFEST talent show live on the internet."

A huge roar of delight filled the school hall.

"The whole world will be watching."

"Eric? ERIC!" shouted Vinnie as Eric's eyes rolled back in his head and a soft moaning sound bubbled out of his mouth.

THE
BARRY CHEESEBALLS
BOX OF MAGIC

"Vinnie Mumbles to Eric Doomsday. Are you receiving me? Over."

The walkie-talkie hissed from somewhere on Eric's bedside table.

Eric picked it up and pushed the button on the side. "I'm here," he said. "Over."

"Are you okay? Over."

"I can't stop thinking about what happened at Hattie's party," Eric replied. "I keep seeing her all covered in cake and bird poo. Every time I think about it, I feel sick. I don't think I can do the talent show. Over."

"Look, you can't let something like that stop you," crackled Vinnie's voice. "You're brilliant at magic, really you are. Like that thing you do with the numbers. Do it again. Do it for me now. Please? Over."

Eric sighed. "Think of a number between one and nine," he said. "Then double it and add eight." He paused for a moment. The walkie-talkie hissed. "Now halve the number and take away your original number," said Eric.

He paused again. "You're now thinking of the number four," he said finally. "Over."

A shriek of delight spluttered out of the walkie-talkie. "*That's what I'm talking about*," Vinnie said. "Honestly, Eric, you're so good at magic, you've got to do it at the talent show. And I've been thinking – just imagine if you won. You'd be so popular. Even Hattie Lavernock would forget about what happened at her birthday party. Over."

"I don't know," said Eric. "I just don't know what to think. OW!" He'd been pacing as he spoke, and he'd stubbed his toe on something hard that was poking out from underneath his bed.

"Eric? Are you okay?" crackled Vinnie's voice.

Eric looked down. "Yeah," he said. "Yeah, I'm fine. Look, I'll call you back in five minutes."

Eric put down the walkie-talkie, reached under his bed and pulled out a large wooden box with gold letters on the top, which said:

BARRY CHEESEBALLS'S BOX OF MAGIC

Barry Cheeseballs was the most popular magician on the internet. His videos of card tricks and illusions that he made in his Palace of Wonder always got millions and millions of views. Eric loved him. It had been watching Barry Cheeseballs videos that had first hooked Eric into magic. And the Christmas before last, Eric's Uncle Jimmy had bought him the Barry Cheeseballs Box of Magic.

Eric slid back the lid and gazed at the treasures within. Coloured silk scarves wrapped themselves around silver cups and packs of crisp, pristine playing cards. He picked up a small blue book that sat at one side of the box. The book had *1001 MAGIC TRICKS TO AMAZE YOUR FAMILY AND FRIENDS* written on it. Eric smiled as he flicked through the book. He stopped at a well-read page that had the title *THE ESSENTIAL SKILLS OF MAGIC* at the top, and saw that he had underlined a sentence in red pen.

MISDIRECTION IS THE SKILL OF MAKING AN AUDIENCE FOCUS ON SOMETHING IN ORDER TO DRAW ATTENTION AWAY FROM SOMETHING ELSE THAT THE MAGICIAN WISHES TO REMAIN SECRET.

One of Eric's favourite card tricks used misdirection. He remembered when he'd done it for the first time one Christmas. He'd got his Auntie Elsie to pick a card from a pack, look at it and then put it face down on the top of the deck. Then Eric misdirected her by asking what the time was. When she looked down at her watch, he took the card from the top of the deck and dropped it in her handbag. When his aunt looked back, Eric showed her that her card had not only mysteriously vanished from the deck but had also reappeared in her handbag. She was amazed at what she saw. Well, she would have been if during the trick's ending, Eric hadn't knocked a whole box of her favourite toffees on the floor, which her dog then ate, before sicking them back up three minutes later all over her favourite white fur rug. No, the look of amazement on her face was quite short-lived. But that didn't matter to Eric because he had been well and truly bitten by the magic bug.

Eric closed the book and placed it carefully back in the box. Then he put the box back under his bed. He thought about what Vinnie had said. Maybe she was right. Maybe if he took part and did his magic and it went well, then everyone would forget about what happened at Hattie Lavernock's birthday party. Maybe he'd stop being a zero.

He turned on his walkie-talkie.

"Eric Doomsday to Vinnie Mumbles. Are you receiving me? Over."

The walkie-talkie hissed for a second.

"*Hearing you loud and clear. Over.*"

"I'm going to do it," said Eric. "I'm going to do the talent show, and I'm going to win."

SMALL TALK

An old grey-haired man noticed the two peculiar-looking individuals who were sitting on a low wall outside Dreary Inkling's doctors' surgery. One of the strangers was wearing a pair of tight, bright green, leather dungarees, and the other was wearing fluorescent pink tracksuit bottoms with a black string vest and gold chains. Both wore bandanas and dark sunglasses, and both were sniffing and poking at large, greasy kebabs from the Mad Doners takeaway shop on the High Street.

"Lovely day," said the man, smiling and politely tipping his hat as he passed.

"WHAT?" said the peculiar-looking stranger in the bright green leather dungarees, throwing his doner kebab in a bin.

"The human is trying to engage us in conversation, Your Mightiness."

"BUT WHAT DOES HE MEAN, 'LOVELY DAY'? THERE'S NOTHING LOVELY ABOUT IT. FOR ONE THING, WE'RE ON A DISGUSTING PLANET WITH A NAME THAT SOUNDS LIKE I'M BEING SICK EVERY TIME I SAY THE WORD. UUURRTH. UUURRTH. AND FOR A SECOND THING, THERE ISN'T ANYTHING DECENT TO EAT HERE."

"Well, Your Mightiness, I believe that the human is performing something known as 'small talk'. The directory mentioned it. It's a human custom."

"SMALL TALK? WHAT'S SMALL TALK?"

"Well, Your Mightiness, according to the directory, 'small talk' is what old humans say when they don't know what to say to other old humans. The three most common topics of 'small talk' are 'the weather', followed by 'how nothing is as good as it used to be', followed by 'the state of my knees'."

His Mightiness looked up at the sky.

"BUT THE WEATHER IS AWFUL TODAY," he said. "IT'S ALL CLOUDY AND WILL PROBABLY RAIN LATER. I MEAN, WHY WOULD YOU SAY

'IT'S A LOVELY DAY' WHEN IT CLEARLY ISN'T A LOVELY DAY AT ALL? IT DOESN'T MAKE ANY SENSE. HE MUST HAVE OUTLIVED HIS USEFULNESS. I'LL VAPORIZE HIM."

But when they turned back, the old grey-haired man had gone. He'd needed a wee quite badly and hadn't wanted to stop and chat to the two peculiar-looking strangers wearing eighties clothes. And besides, he'd forgotten to put his hearing aid in and so hadn't heard a single word they had said.

TUESDAY

THE "WHEN IS A MYSTICAL MOUSE OF MYSTERY NOT A MYSTICAL MOUSE OF MYSTERY?" MYSTERY

Eric sat in Vinnie's bedroom and stared into the little brown eyes of Vinnie's hamster, Steve Enjoy. Steve Enjoy stared back at him, then nibbled on a small slice of apple and ran behind his wheel.

"I love Steve Enjoy," said Eric.

"Do not call him Steve Enjoy," said Vinnie.

"From now on, he is Mr Magique, the Mystical Mouse of Mystery."

"Vinnie!" shouted Vinnie's mum from downstairs. "Time for school."

"But he's a hamster, not a mouse," said Eric, as he and Vinnie completely ignored Vinnie's mum.

"Well, you try finding adjectives about magic that begin with 'h'," said Vinnie. "No one will know. He looks a bit mousey."

Eric agreed that Steve Enjoy did have a certain mouseish look about him.

"Listen," said Vinnie. "Your magic is great, but if you want to win the DRIPSFEST talent show your act needs to be great too. You need to have something that is going to blow people's minds. And Mr Magique is going to do that for you."

"How?" said Eric.

"Well, I thought you could wheel his cage onto the stage and make him disappear or saw him in half or something like that. You know, like magicians do."

Eric looked at Vinnie. "Make him disappear? Saw him in half?" he said. "To do either of those things I'd need to get a special cabinet built, with mirrors on the inside, and a false floor and stuff like that. It'd take weeks to sort out and we've only got a day."

"Oh," said Vinnie. "Could you pull him out of a hat?"

Eric watched as Steve Enjoy ran into one corner of the cage, then scrambled onto his wheel, then scurried down a tube.

"Nah, hamsters move around too much," he said. "The reason magicians use rabbits is because they lie still. Barry Cheeseballs did a video on it."

"Oh," said Vinnie.

"VINNIE!" shouted Vinnie's mum again, a bit louder this time. "It's time for school. Come on."

"So you can't use him at all?" said Vinnie, ignoring her mum again.

Eric rubbed his chin.

"I didn't say that," he said, grabbing a pack of cards from his school bag. "There might be something we could do." He opened up the pack and tipped the deck out into his hand, sneaking a glance at the bottom card.

Vinnie's eyes lit up. "What?"

"Well, how about this?" said Eric, writing

something on a piece of paper and putting it inside Steve Enjoy's cage. Steve Enjoy scuttled up to the piece of paper, sniffed it and ran back to his piece of apple. Eric took the deck of cards and fanned them out.

"Pick any card," he said.

Vinnie picked a card, and Eric showed her the card she'd picked.

"Queen of spades," she said.

"Now have a look what's on the piece of paper," said Eric, pointing to the cage.

Vinnie slowly opened up the hatch at the top of the cage and grabbed the bit of paper that Eric had written on. She unfolded it and right there, in Eric's handwriting, were the words Queen of spades. Vinnie's jaw nearly hit the floor.

"How did you do that?" she said.

Eric smiled. "I just looked at the bottom card before the trick. The prediction is whatever the bottom card is. Then all I had to do was make sure you picked the bottom card."

"But I didn't pick the bottom card," said Vinnie.

"Well, I had moved it," said Eric. "It's called a 'card force'. It's where I force you to pick the card I want you to pick."

"How did you do *that*?" said Vinnie, a look of astonishment on her face.

Eric tapped the side of his nose. "Practice," he said. "Lots of practice."

Vinnie looked at Eric and shook her head. "Brilliant."

Eric shuffled the cards and put them back in the pack. "So, what are you going to do for the talent show?" he said.

"Oh, just a short presentation I've been working on," said Vinnie.

"About space?" said Eric.

Vinnie nodded. "Yeah, just something I knocked up the other day."

"Cool," said Eric. "What's it called?"

"*How Titanium Isotopes Provide Clues to the Origin of the Moon*," said Vinnie. "It's pretty basic stuff and I've practically written it already, so I'll have bags of time to help you."

Eric, who hadn't understood a single word of what Vinnie had just said other than moon, nodded.

"VINNIE!" screamed Vinnie's mum. "GET DOWN HERE NOW OR YOU'LL BE LATE!"

Vinnie opened the door of her room. "Alright, alright," she called. "We're coming, Mum, there's no need to shout."

ERIC'S
NEW TRICK

When they got to school, Eric and Vinnie made their way to morning assembly, only to discover that all lessons had been cancelled. Instead, Mrs Tittering was handing out jobs to all classes to help get the school ready for DRIPSFEST.

The Reception class had to dust all the classrooms – Mrs Tittering said that their tiny, tiny hands meant they could reach further behind the radiators with their dusters than any other children. Year One were given the task of filling in the potholes on the playground with soil and planting flowers in them. Classes from Years Two and Three were put on a strict mopping detail, whereby Mrs Tittering attached mop-heads to their hands and knees and made them crawl around the school until they had cleaned every floor.

Years Four and Five were made to mow the sports field, repaint the racetrack, fill the long-jump pit with sand and make sure there were enough sacks, skipping ropes and miniature beanbags for all the DRIPSFEST Olympic events. Finally, only the Year Six class was left.

"Right then, I want you lot to get yourselves ready for the talent show," said Mrs Tittering. "We're going to be having some special guests

watching, so it's really important that you're absolutely perfect tomorrow. So that means practice, practice, practice. Between now and tomorrow morning's assembly that's all I want you to do. Well, that and clean the toilets. I've organized a rota."

Mrs Tittering looked at Eric and Vinnie. "You two have the first shift," she said, thrusting a mop, bucket and a bag of cleaning implements into their hands. "The rest of you get back to your classrooms and get practising."

A few minutes later, Eric and Vinnie were standing just outside the door of the girls' toilets.

"Brace yourself," said Vinnie. "Because what you are about to see you will never be able to unsee."

Eric nodded. He had always wanted to know what the insides of the girls' toilets looked like, but had never dared think he would find out. Vinnie slowly pushed open the door and the pair walked inside.

"W-what...o-on...E-Earth?" he stuttered.

Eric had known it was going to be different, but he hadn't dreamed it would be this different.

"Y-y-y-your paper towel dispenser," he said, gawping at the wall. "It's on the left-hand side of the mirror, not the right-hand side."

Vinnie pursed her lips and nodded. "Get used to it, Doomsday, you're not in the boys' toilets now."

Eric did not feel at all comfortable being in the girls' toilets. It was like he had stepped into another dimension where everything sort

111

of looked the same but actually was completely weird and different, like a world where people ate through their eyes or wore socks made of cheese. He started mopping the floor as quickly as he could. He didn't want to stay in this strange new land a second longer than he had to.

"So, talk me through your routine," said Vinnie on her hands and knees as she scrubbed the floor around a toilet with a toothbrush.

"Well," said Eric. "I thought I'd start by vanishing some silk scarves."

"Okay," said Vinnie.

"Then I'll do a card trick with Mr Magique," said Eric.

"Good idea," said Vinnie.

"And then I thought I'd finish with something new."

Vinnie stopped scrubbing. "Something new," she said. "What is it? Show me."

Eric smiled and put down his mop. Then he grabbed a plastic cup, a small piece of cardboard and a flask out of his school bag.

"Right," he said. "Here goes. So I've got this cup—"

"STOP!" yelled Vinnie.

"What?"

"I've told you, if you want to win the contest then your act has got to be exciting, and already this is way too boring. You need some PIZZAZZ. Have you got a black cape?"

"Er, no!" said Eric.

"Top hat?"

"No."

"Flashing shoes?"

"NO!"

Vinnie thought for a moment. "Okay, well I'll have a look at home tonight for some stuff. I'm sure my mum has a sparkly coat she wouldn't mind me borrowing. I'll bring it in tomorrow. Okay, continue."

Eric picked up the glass and showed it to Vinnie. He knew it was important to show off the props to the audience to give them the impression that everything was completely normal. Next, he filled the glass with water from the flask.

"STOP!" yelled Vinnie.

"What?" said Eric.

"Water is just too boring and you can't see it properly. Use something else, like orange juice or water with dye in it. Bung in some glitter or hundreds and thousands, or something like that. Make it all sparkly. Okay? Continue."

Eric picked up the small piece of cardboard and showed it to Vinnie. The cardboard was a bit bigger than the mouth of the glass.

"STOP!" yelled Vinnie.

"What now?" said Eric.

"What is that?"

"It's a piece of cardboard," said Eric.

"I know it's a piece of cardboard," Vinnie sighed. "And pieces of cardboard look boring." She thought for a moment. "Have you got some sparkly wrapping paper you could cover it in?"

"Yeah, I suppose," said Eric.

"Good, that'll look much better. Now, continue."

Eric put the cardboard square on top of the glass and turned the glass and the card upside down. Then, keeping hold of the glass, he took his hands away from the cardboard. Incredibly, and as if by magic, the cardboard stuck to the glass, holding the water in despite the glass being upside down.

"Hmmmmmm," said Vinnie. "It's okay, I suppose, but it's pretty obvious the cardboard is being held up by suction."

But Eric wasn't finished. He smiled and then did something *really* magic. He pulled the cardboard away from the still-upside-down glass and, as if defying gravity, the water did not fall

116

but remained where
it was, seemingly
floating in the glass.

Vinnie cheered
and whistled. "Eric,
that's amazing!"
she said.

Eric smiled and
turned the glass the
right way up.

"How did you DO that?"
said Vinnie.

Eric pulled a small disc of clear plastic from
the top of the glass.

"It's on the cardboard," he said. "So when I take
the cardboard away, the plastic sticks to the glass

and the water doesn't fall out. It's pretty simple really."

"That is a killer routine," said Vinnie. "On the night though, why don't you hold the glass over someone's head? A teacher or someone like that. Then everyone would think the teacher was going to get a soaking. It would add some drama to the trick."

"Good idea," said Eric.

"And you definitely need to have an amazing ending. Remember, you've got to blow people's minds."

Eric nodded and pulled three small round balls out of his bag.

"I'm going to use these," he said.

"What are they?"

"They're smoke bombs," said Eric. "I'm going to throw them on the floor before I leave the stage. When they explode they'll create a large plume of smoke. It's a bit of misdirection really – everyone will be looking at the smoke while I get off the stage. It'll look like I completely vanish. Magicians call it a Big Spectacular Exit."

"Perfect," said Vinnie. "You know what, Eric Doomsday? I've got a really good feeling about this."

Eric smiled and they both did their special secret smile where they curled their fingers around their top lips like moustaches and opened their eyes as wide as they would go.

WEDNESDAY

DRIPSFEST DAY

Little bubbles of excited chatter popped and winked around the school hall.

"Who are they?" whispered Vinnie, nodding towards two strange-looking people who were sitting onstage next to Mrs Tittering.

"Search me," said Eric.

Each stranger had enormous permed hair with a lime green headband stretched around it. Across their noses they had a thick stripe of white make-

121

up and they both wore massive trousers that seemed to be made out of parachute material. The strange-looking man on the left had a neon pink T-shirt with a smiley face on the front, and the strange-looking man on the right had a pair of glittery antennae on his head that bobbled around as he moved. And to top off their bizarre clothing choices, each wore a pair of large dark glasses.

Mrs Tittering stood and held up her hands for silence.

"Thank you, thank you," she said in that way teachers say *Thank you, thank you* when you know what they really mean is *Shut up, shut up.* "Good morning, children."

"Good mor-ning, Mis-sus Ti-tter-ing, good

mor-ning, ev-ery-bod-y," said the whole school together, in a way that sounded like each and every one of them had had the life sucked out of their souls.

"I would like to introduce you all to two very special visitors this morning," said Mrs Tittering.

The two odd-looking people stood up.

"They are inspectors who have come to look at the school. So, they will be coming around throughout the day to see what everyone is doing. And I have asked both the inspectors if they will help me judge the Year Six talent show this morning."

The inspector with the neon T-shirt held up his hands as if to address the school. "HELLO, PUNY HUMANS," he said.

The other inspector, who was standing right
next to him, whispered in his ear.

The inspector wearing the neon T-shirt nodded.
"OH YES, OF COURSE. I MEAN, HELLO, PUNY
CHILDREN."

The other inspector whispered something else
in his ear.

"REALLY?" said the inspector in the neon
T-shirt. "BUT THEY ARE SO PUNY."

The other inspector whispered something else
in his ear.

"OH, VERY WELL," sighed the inspector in the neon T-shirt. "HELLO, CHILDREN."

The other inspector nodded and smiled.

"Well, er, thank you, er, Mr, er...oh dear me, I've just realized that I don't know your names," said Mrs Tittering.

"OH, YES, OUR NAMES," said the inspector wearing the neon T-shirt. "WELL, OUR NAMES ARE JUST COMPLETELY NORMAL NAMES THAT ANYONE WOULD HAVE ON THIS STUPID PLANET."

"Yes?" said Mrs Tittering.

The other inspector whispered something. As he did, he pointed at a sign on the wall.

"ER, MY NAME," said the inspector with the neon T-shirt, "MY PERFECTLY NORMAL

HUMAN NAME IS DON O'TENTER."

"Good mor-ning, Don-O-Tenter, good mor-ning, ev-ery-bod-y," sang the school.

"Don O'Tenter?" whispered Vinnie to Eric. "That's a very strange name."

"They are very strange people," whispered Eric. "I mean, look at their trousers."

"Welcome to the school, Mr O'Tenter," said Mrs Tittering. "And what is your colleague's name?"

"WHAT?" said Mr O'Tenter, who clearly hadn't been expecting to have to come up with two names.

"His name is Mr Watt?" said Mrs Tittering.

"WHAT?" said Mr O'Tenter.

Mrs Tittering scratched her head. "His name is Mr Watt-Watt?" she said.

"What?" said the other inspector.

"WHAT?" said Mr O'Tenter.

"Wait, he's called Mr Watt-Watt-Watt-Watt?" said Mrs Tittering.

Mr O'Tenter turned and looked at the other inspector. "YES," he said, clearly wanting to bring this naming ordeal to an end.

"Good mor-ning, Mis-ter Watt-Watt-Watt-Watt, good mor-ning, ev-ery-bod-y," sang the school.

Mrs Tittering looked a little puzzled but, then again, school inspectors were always a bit weird. She thought it best to try and move the day along.

"Well, Mr O'Tenter, Mr Watt-Watt-Watt-Watt," she said. "You've timed your visit perfectly, because today is the day that we hold the Dreary

Inkling Primary School Festival. It's a perfect opportunity to see the very best of the school."

She pulled out a crumpled bit of paper from her pocket and read from it.

"DRIPSFEST is a day where creativity, learning and athletic achievement are all encouraged and celebrated. A day where we can show how this school nurtures and develops the talent of our pupils."

The inspectors turned and looked at each other, narrowing their eyes suspiciously.

"So, to get things started," continued Mrs Tittering, "we will have the special Year Six DRIPSFEST talent show assembly. It'll be a chance for you to see the very finest talent that Dreary Inkling has to offer."

"THE VERY FINEST?" said Mr O'Tenter. "ARE YOU SURE?"

"Oh yes," said Mrs Tittering. "Some of our Year Six pupils are extremely talented. So without further ado, let's begin DRIPSFEST."

A huge cheer erupted around the school hall.

Mr Don O'Tenter turned to Mr Watt-Watt-Watt-Watt.

"THESE HUMAN CHILDREN HAD BETTER BE GOOD," he whispered. "BECAUSE THE INSPECTION OF THEIR SPECIES HAS NOT GONE VERY WELL SO FAR. IN FACT, YOU COULD SAY THAT THIS LOT ARE THE HUMANS' VERY LAST HOPE."

Mr Watt-Watt-Watt-Watt nodded and smiled.

"Yes, Your Mightiness."

THE YEAR SIX DRIPSFEST TALENT SHOW

Eric sat next to Vinnie on the bench at the back of the stage, alongside all his Year Six classmates nervously waiting for the talent show to begin. He drummed his fingers on his leg and listened as the rumble of excited chatter grew louder and louder.

"Here you go," said Vinnie, handing him a small cage draped in a sparkly cloth. Eric peeked into the cage and saw Mr Magique nibbling a nut.

"Is he okay?" said Eric.

"Of course he's okay," said Vinnie.

"He's got magic flowing through those paws."

Eric put the cloth back over the top and placed the cage carefully under his seat. Then Vinnie passed Eric a canvas bag.

"What's this?" he said.

"Your costume," said Vinnie. "I pulled together a few things we had in our house. It took me most of last night."

Eric opened the bag and peered inside. "You've got to be kidding me," he said.

"What?" said Vinnie.

"I can't wear that."

"It'll make you look more like a top magician," said Vinnie.

"It won't," said Eric. "It'll make me look like a top loser. It looks ridicul—"

"QUIET!" screamed Mrs Tittering, standing at the front of the stage. She gave the thumbs up to Mr Flange, who was waiting in the wings. He nodded, then pushed up his large, thick glasses on top of his head and held up his phone, ready to film.

"And we'll be live-streaming the DRIPSFEST talent show in three, two, one..." he said, tapping the record button. He glanced at the counter in the corner of the screen and saw that there were three people watching.

Mrs Tittering smoothed down her hair and smiled nervously into Mr Flange's phone. She wanted more than anything for DRIPSFEST to become an internet sensation, because there was no way the council would be able to close down an internet sensation.

"It is with the greatest pleasure," she began, "that I welcome everyone here at Dreary Inkling Primary School, as well as everyone watching online, to the DRIPSFEST talent show."

The audience applauded and Mr Flange got a lovely shot of the Year Three pupils cheering loudly. He glanced at the counter in the corner of the screen again. There were now two people watching.

"The judging of the talent show will be very simple," continued Mrs Tittering. "Myself and our special guest judges, Mr O'Tenter and Mr Watt-Watt-Watt-Watt each have paddles with numbers on, just like the judges on the telly. So, once the act has finished, we will hold up the number that demonstrates how we feel about the act. Although I'm sure that all our performers will get high scores."

Mrs Tittering chuckled and looked over at Mr O'Tenter and Mr Watt-Watt-Watt-Watt, who were now sitting at the judging table at the side of the stage. They did not chuckle. They just stared straight back at her.

"Er, well, so without further ado," continued Mrs Tittering, "let the talent show begin! And our first act is Tom Boosbeck."

Mrs Tittering took her seat next to Mr O'Tenter and Mr Watt-Watt-Watt-Watt as Tom Boosbeck walked out onto the stage holding a trumpet and a music stand. He arranged some sheets of music on the stand and got ready to play a short piece that he had composed himself called "The Boosbeck Boogie". Taking a deep breath, he looked out into the audience, then brought the trumpet to his lips and blew.

It was the best performance
Tom had ever given –
but almost as soon
as the first squeaky
note came out of the
trumpet, Mr O'Tenter and
Mr Watt-Watt-Watt-Watt
clamped their hands over

their ears and began screaming, "NO! NO! NO!"
Bravely, Tom ignored the distraction and finished
the piece, and the audience gave him a warm
round of applause as he took a bow.

"THANK GOODNESS THAT AWFUL RACKET HAS STOPPED," said Mr O'Tenter in a very loud voice. "THAT WAS TERRIBLE."

The audience fell silent.

"Now, just hang on a minute," said Mrs Tittering, who was more than a little shocked at how harsh the inspectors were being. "Tom has only been playing the trumpet for a few months." She turned to Tom, holding up an "8". "I thought you did a wonderful job, Tom. I suppose some music is not to everyone's taste."

The audience cheered.

"YOU'RE RIGHT," said Mr O'Tenter. "IT WASN'T TO MY TASTE BECAUSE IT SOUNDED LIKE SOMEONE WAS SCRAPING THE INSIDES OF MY BRAIN OUT AND BEING SICK INSIDE MY HEAD."

The audience gasped.

Mr O'Tenter and Mr Watt-Watt-Watt-Watt both held up a "1". And they only gave that because they hadn't been given any lower numbers.

Tom took his trumpet and wandered offstage, sobbing. Mrs Tittering bit her nails. She did not like the way things were going and had a terrible feeling in the pits of her gut that things were going to get even worse. And Mrs Tittering's gut pits had never been wrong before.

THE INSPECTION CORRECTION

"When are you on?" whispered Vinnie to Eric as Luis Agueda took to the stage.

"I'm on last," said Eric.

"When are you going to get your outfit on?" said Vinnie.

"Later," he said. "Much, much later."

Luis Agueda was dressed entirely in black. He had been practising mime for a few years and loved performing for a crowd.

"He's very good," whispered Mrs Tittering to Mr O'Tenter and Mr Watt-Watt-Watt-Watt. "One of the favourites, I would say."

Luis had decided he was going to perform his most ambitious and complicated routine. His performance began with his mime of a boy blown by the wind. Next, he performed his mime of a boy walking a dog, before building to a thrilling climax of a boy trapped in a glass box with a swarm of killer bees. He pulled it off perfectly and the audience cheered and applauded loudly.

Mrs Tittering allowed herself a tiny smile. "That was excellent," she said and held up a "9".

The audience cheered again.

Mrs Tittering allowed her tiny smile to grow a bit bigger.

"WELL, I THOUGHT THAT WAS SICKENING AND REVOLTING," said Mr O'Tenter.

The cheering stopped dead.

"I agree," said Mr Watt-Watt-Watt-Watt, who had drawn a decimal point in between the 1 and the 0 of his "10" paddle and then turned it upside down so it read 0.1. "Appalling and shocking."

Some of the older pupils booed a bit at this and Nancy Goonhaven from Year Five even stood up and shouted "STOP BEING MEAN!" at the inspectors. However, Mr O'Tenter glared at her so ferociously that it looked like his eyes were glowing red behind his sunglasses. Nancy immediately sat down, and after that no one said another word.

The next forty-five minutes were awful for the

142

pupils and staff of Dreary Inkling Primary School. As each new act performed, the two inspectors became more and more rude. Everything was "HOPELESS" or "DISGUSTING" or "PATHETIC" or "FEEBLE" or "APPALLING". The inspectors even said that Betty Gabalfa's performance had "BROUGHT SHAME TO THE ENTIRE HUMAN RACE". This seemed especially harsh, as Betty's act had involved jumping over a huge tank of stick insects, on roller skates, while reciting the alphabet backwards, in French.

There were a couple of bright spots. Vinnie's *How Titanium Isotopes Provide Clues to the Origin of the Moon* presentation got two scores of "7" from Mr O'Tenter and Mr Watt-Wall-Watt-Watt, who both, for a brief moment, seemed quite impressed. And Hattie Lavernock's talking parrot act received a "6" and a "5", although this was because Hattie's parrot had repeated the third-worst swear word in the world fifteen times in a row and then done a huge plop on Mrs Tittering's head, which both Mr O'Tenter and Mr Watt-Watt-Watt-Watt thought was hilarious.

Soon though, just two acts remained: Eddie Splott and Eric. But as Eddie took to the stage and started to shoot peas out of his nose into a bucket, the school secretary, Mrs Fesnying, rushed into the hall with another woman.

"Mrs Tittering? Mrs Tittering?" she called, and dashed over to the judges' table. Eric watched as the other woman followed behind, her shoes clattering on the hard wooden floor of the hall.

She was small and round and wore the tiniest glasses, which made her eyes look like raisins.

"What is it?" said Mrs Tittering.

"Er, this is Ms Lotte," said Mrs Fesnying. "Ms P.A. Lotte, from the council."

The reception pupils in the front row sniggered when they heard Ms Lotte's name.

"Er, Ms Lotte, yes, er, hello," said Mrs Tittering, leaping up from her chair. "Welcome to Dreary Inkling Primary School."

Ms Lotte's tiny eyes scanned the room.

"The DRIPSFEST talent show has nearly finished I'm afraid, but your two colleagues have been, er, enjoying it."

Ms Lotte looked at Mr O'Tenter and Mr Watt-Watt-Watt-Watt.

"They are not my colleagues," she said. "I've just spoken to my colleagues. They broke down on the motorway and so I'll have to do the inspection on my own. I have never seen these two people before in my life."

Everyone in the hall had stopped watching Eddie Splott firing peas out of his nose and was now watching Mrs Tittering. She turned and looked at Mr O'Tenter and Mr Watt-Watt-Watt-Watt, who both stood up. Mrs Tittering gulped. They seemed a lot taller than she remembered.

"B-but...if you're not here to inspect our school, then who are you? And why are you here?"

Mr O'Tenter pointed at Mr Flange's live-streaming phone and a strange blue lightning crackled out of his finger and hit it. Mr Flange looked at the counter in the corner of the screen.

It had suddenly shot up from 5 to 3,466,108,799.

"OH, WE'RE NOT HERE TO INSPECT YOUR
SCHOOL," said Mr O'Tenter. "WE'RE HERE TO
INSPECT YOUR WHOLE SPECIES."

ANIMALS DOING THE FUNNIEST THINGS WEARING PEOPLE'S UNDERWEAR

The Prime Minister sat sprawled across the seventh largest sofa in the world, his eyes glued to an enormous television in the corner of his office. No one on the face of the planet was a bigger fan of *Animals Doing the Funniest Things Wearing People's Underwear* than him. He loved it. In fact, he'd even sent a video to the show when he'd filmed an otter wearing a pair of ceremonial Brazilian marching pants that he'd been given on a state visit. Obviously, he'd had to make sure you couldn't tell it was him, because Prime Ministers were definitely not supposed to make otters wear their undergarments, ceremonial marching pants or no ceremonial marching pants.

As the *Animals Doing the Funniest Things Wearing People's Underwear* theme music started to play, the PM cracked open a jumbo packet of Señor Fundillos Cheesy Chilli-breath Tortilla Chips.

"This is the life," he said, using a rare eighteenth-century gold soup ladle to shovel some chips from the bag into his mouth. On the enormous TV screen, a man had dressed up a couple of hamsters to look like famous singers and had just popped them in a pair of tights.

"Now that," chuckled the PM, spewing fragments of nacho chip onto the sofa, "is top-notch telly."

But *Animals Doing the Funniest Things Wearing People's Underwear* had barely been on for three minutes when the picture on the massive telly changed. Suddenly all the Prime Minister could see was a face. The face of an odd-looking person with colossal permed hair and wearing large dark glasses. It was the face of Mr O'Tenter.

"What the—?" spluttered the Prime Minister.

He picked up the remote control and flicked to another channel. But the face kept staring back at him. He flicked to yet another channel, but the face was still there.

And the Prime Minister wasn't the only person seeing Mr O'Tenter's face. Because the strange

blue lightning that had shot out of the inspector's fingers had started broadcasting the footage from Mr Flange's phone to every single screen in the world. On every smartphone, on every tablet, on every TV in every home and shop, on every computer screen in every bedroom and office, and on every movie screen in every cinema across the planet. From Addis Ababa to Zagreb and from Australia to Zaire, everyone looking at a screen was watching Mr O'Tenter in the hall of Dreary Inkling Primary School.

"PEOPLE OF THE PLANET UUURRTH. YOU HAVE BEEN INSPECTED AND YOU HAVE FAILED. PREPARE TO BE DESTROYED."

E-DARD Oo-DARD AND TREVOR

"M-M-Mr O'Tenter," said Mrs Tittering. "W-what is g-going on?"

"I AM NOT MR DON O'TENTER," said Mr Don O'Tenter, looking straight into the camera. "I SIMPLY MADE UP THAT NAME FROM THE SIGN ON THE WALL BECAUSE I'M SO BRILLIANT." He pointed to the *Do Not Enter* sign by the wall bars. "I AM NOT OF THIS WORLD. BEHOLD MY TRUE FORM."

Eric, Vinnie and the rest of the humans in the school hall watched as Mr O'Tenter began snarling and frothing at the mouth. He pulled off his tightly permed hair and headband and threw them on the floor. Then he took off his dark glasses to reveal two red eyes that burned like embers from the fires of hell.

Eric gasped.

He'd seen those eyes before.

Mr O'Tenter (or whatever it was that had been calling itself Mr O'Tenter) reached around behind its head and began fiddling with something. He tutted to himself as he fiddled, before eventually turning to face Mr Watt-Watt-Watt-Watt.

"WOULD YOU MIND?" he slobbered.

Mr Watt-Watt-Watt-Watt walked over and put

his hand on the back of whatever it was that had been calling itself Mr O'Tenter's neck.

"Certainly, Your Mightiness," he said and began to tug at something, grunting and huffing while he did.

"GIVE IT A REALLY GOOD PULL. GO ON. PUT YOUR BACK INTO IT."

"It. Appears. To. Be. Stuck. Your. Mightiness," said Mr Watt-Watt-Watt-Watt. "Perhaps. It's. A. Bit. Too. Small?"

"OF COURSE IT'S NOT TOO SMALL! OR ARE YOU TRYING TO TELL ME THAT I'VE PUT ON WEIGHT?"

"Oh, er, absolutely not, Your Mightiness, you are in peak physical condition," said Mr Watt-Watt-Watt-Watt, who pulled and yanked until, with one last big grunt, all the skin on the body and face of the creature that had been calling itself Mr O'Tenter fell down onto the floor with a *FFFFFLUMP*.

Eric and the rest of Dreary Inkling Primary School looked on in horror as a terrifying creature stepped out of the skin like it was a discarded onesie. Red eyes burned from a large elongated skull with pale, papery skin stretched over it so tight that Eric could see a brain twitching and pulsating underneath. The creature's body was long and its muscles and sinews quivered on the outside of its huge arms and legs. It was dark grey in colour, and its whole body glistened, like it had been dipped in a bath of slime. It stood there for a moment, breathing

noisily, before it dropped onto all fours and began prowling around the stage, never once taking its eyes off Mr Flange's phone, which was still live-streaming to the world.

All around the hall, gasps of shock gave way to cries for help. Eric wanted to run, but his legs seemed to have stopped working. All he could do was watch as most of Dreary Inkling Primary School's teachers and pupils made a panicked rush for the doors. But before they could get there, the creature held up a long-taloned hand and the doors to the hall all slammed shut, locking everyone inside.

Next, Mr Watt-Watt-Watt-Watt, or whatever it was that had been calling itself Mr Watt-Watt-Watt-Watt, unzipped itself from the skin suit it had been wearing and revealed its similar, but no less terrifying, self. There were more gasps of horror. Eric looked around and saw Hattie Lavernock and Grace Smeaton clinging on to each other, looks of utter terror plastered on their faces. Eddie Splott and Tom Boosbeck were trembling behind the bench at the back of the stage. Ms Mustering and Mrs Fesnying were hammering with their fists on the door.

Eric turned to his best friend. "What's happening?" he spluttered.

"Fascinating," whispered Vinnie, who didn't seem the slightest bit frightened. "This is actual contact with an alien race. I wonder if they're a carbon-based or a silicon-based life form?"

The creature that had unzipped its skin first

continued prowling around the stage.

"MY REAL NAME IS E-DARD OO-DARD," he snarled, slime slobbering from his mouth and splattering around the hall. "I AM THE SUPREME AND MIGHTY LEADER OF THE GALAXY INSPECTORS FROM THE PLANET VALRIK. AND THIS IS MY NUMBER TWO, TREVOR."

"Hello," said Trevor.

"Sorry, what planet are you from?" said Mrs Tittering, who was now slumped in a chair, fanning herself with a DRIPSFEST programme.

"THE PLANET VALRIK!" screamed E-Dard Oo-Dard.

"Valrik!" repeated Trevor.

"Oh," said Mrs Tittering. "I've not heard of that."

"WHAT DO YOU MEAN, YOU'VE NOT HEARD

OF VALRIK? YOU MUST HAVE HEARD OF VALRIK!"

Mrs Tittering looked E-Dard Oo-Dard in the eye nervously.

"Er, no," she said. "I don't think I have."

"BUT VALRIK IS THE MOST FAMOUS PLANET IN THE GALAXY. OUR WARRIOR RACE IS FEARED AMONG THE SEVEN NEBULAS OF NOTWEN THEAH, AND THE SPIRAL ARM OF DETINU NAM, AND THE THREE STARS OF CANTONA."

"Cantona!" repeated Trevor.

Mrs Tittering shook her head. "Sorry," she squeaked.

"SILENCE!" shrieked E-Dard Oo-Dard. "IT DOES NOT MATTER, IT IS MERELY FURTHER

EVIDENCE THAT ON THE LIST OF GALACTIC
INTELLIGENCE, YOUR SPECIES COMES
BOTTOM."

"Bottom!" repeated Trevor.

E-Dard Oo-Dard turned around and snarled at
Trevor. "WILL YOU STOP REPEATING
EVERYTHING? IT'S VERY ANNOYING," he
said. "AND YOU'VE MADE ME FORGET WHAT
I WAS SAYING. WHERE WAS I?"

Vinnie put up her hand.

"WHAT?" snapped
E-Dard Oo-Dard.

"Er, you were just saying how humans were at the bottom of galactic intelligence," she said.

"OH, YES, THAT'S RIGHT, THANK YOU," said E-Dard Oo-Dard. "IT IS THE JOB OF THE GALAXY INSPECTORS TO TRAVEL AROUND THE MILKY WAY, INSPECTING ALL INTELLIGENT LIFE FORMS TO MAKE SURE THEY ARE WORTHY OF THE GIFT OF LIFE. ANY LIFE FORMS THAT FAIL THE INSPECTION ARE ELIMINATED TO MAKE WAY FOR OTHERS. AND, AS YOU ARE AT THE BOTTOM OF GALACTIC INTELLIGENCE, WE ARE GOING TO KILL YOU ALL."

"ALL," repeated Trevor but very, very quietly so only he could really hear.

THE PRIME MINISTER'S BRILLIANT PLAN

Just ten minutes after he had seen the alien broadcast, the Prime Minister's study was full of all the country's top military and scientific experts. The Prime Minister's aides had set up a huge bank of phones, each with a secure line to one of the world's other top leaders.

In fact, his study was now so noisy that the Prime Minister was finding it very difficult to concentrate. There were people shouting all around him about military strategies and the DNA structure of the aliens and whether he should make a speech to the nation. Everyone wanted to talk to him all at once, and it seemed as if there was a never-ending stream of questions for him to answer. Finally, he had had enough.

"Something must be done," he said, standing up with great purpose. The room fell silent. The Prime Minister scrunched up the now empty packet of Señor Fundillos Cheesy Chilli-breath Tortilla Chips and tossed it onto the seventeenth-century, hand-woven Persian rug on the floor.

"Er, absolutely, Prime Minister," said Field Marshall Horsell. "But what can we do?"

The Prime Minister sighed. "Well, there is something we could try," he said.

The Field Marshall leaned in closer. "Yes?" he said.

"It's not going to be easy," said the Prime Minister, "but now is not the time for us to stand by and do nothing and hope against hope that others will come to our aid. Now is the time for us to act. Now is the time for us to be strong. Now is the time for us to be heroes!"

The study erupted in applause and cheers at these great and inspiring words from the Prime Minister.

"What is it?" said the Field Marshall. "What, what, WHAT?"

"Well," said the Prime Minister, "I think that you should come up with a plan to get rid of the aliens."

There was a silence.

"Yes," said the Field Marshall. "But how?"

"Oh, I don't know, just build some kind of super-rockety-anti-alien-bazookary-thingy, or something. You'll work it out."

The Field Marshall rolled his eyes and sighed.

"So, Prime Minister," he said, eventually, "your plan was for us to come up with a plan."

"That's the plan," said the Prime Minister. "You can thank me when this is all over. Now, has anyone tried to get the telly back on?"

SPOONFINGERS

E-Dard Oo-Dard, the supreme and mighty leader of the Galaxy Inspectors from the planet Valrik and the creature formerly known as Mr Don O'Tenter, pushed himself up until he was standing on just his hind legs. He stalked around the Dreary Inkling Primary School stage, flexing his long fingers, his sharp talons glinting in the talent show stage lighting.

"I think that is what made those scratches on

our fence," whispered Eric to Vinnie.

Vinnie nodded. "Agreed," she whispered back. "And they seem to be as comfortable on two legs as four. Like a bear. Or a performing dog. Their skeletal structure must be fascinating."

E-Dard Oo-Dard looked directly into Mr Flange's live-streaming phone.

"FOR THE LAST THREE DAYS," he said, "WE HAVE BEEN OBSERVING AND ASSESSING ALL HUMANS WITHIN THE RANDOMLY CHOSEN INSPECTION ZONE OF DREARY INKLING."

He paused and a long, forked tongue whipped out of his mouth and licked his ear. Eric could see the alien's enormous brain pulsating inside his head.

"AFTER OUR INSPECTION, WE HAVE SEEN NOTHING TO MAKE US THINK THAT YOUR SPECIES IS WORTHY OF HAVING LIFE. YOU ARE EVEN MORE DIM-WITTED THAN THE COLOSSALLY STUPID GRAHAM BUMSTEADS FROM THE MOONS OF LOOP PREVIL. AND I THOUGHT THAT WOULD BE IMPOSSIBLE."

E-Dard Oo-Dard paused again.

"AND SO, UNDER SECTION 250599 OF THE INTERGALACTIC CONVENTION, ALL HUMANS WILL BE VAPORIZED. THANK YOU."

There was silence in the Dreary Inkling school hall and across the globe as the words of E-Dard Oo-Dard, the supreme and mighty leader of the Galaxy Inspectors from the planet Valrik, sank in.

"Wait!" said Vinnie from the back of the stage.

"You can't do this. It's not fair."

E-Dard Oo-Dard stalked over to where Eric and Vinnie were standing.

"OH, IT'S VERY FAIR," he slobbered. "WE ALWAYS DO EVERYTHING BY THE BOOK. THE INTERGALACTIC CONVENTION INSISTS UPON IT. TELL THEM, TREVOR." E-Dard Oo-Dard clicked his fingers.

"We always follow the same procedure that we have followed for the last three million years," said Trevor. "When we evaluate a species, we randomly pick a small area of the planet and look at four key areas of intelligence - namely, technology, food and children."

"That's three key areas," said Eric.

"WHAT?" said E-Dard Oo-Dard.

"He said technology, food and children. That's only three key areas, not four."

E-Dard Oo-Dard sighed and hit Trevor on the

side of his head. "YOU'RE MAKING US LOOK VERY UNPROFESSIONAL," he said.

"Er, sorry, Your Mightiness," Trevor said.

E-Dard Oo-Dard turned back to look at Eric and Vinnie. "WELL, IT DOESN'T REALLY MATTER HOW MANY KEY AREAS THERE ARE, BECAUSE HUMANS FAILED IN ALL OF THEM. AND THAT IS WHY YOU WILL BE VAPORIZED."

"But we can't have failed," said Eric. "Not all of them."

"Yeah," said Vinnie. "We've got some great technology, for a start. We've built spacecrafts and telescopes that can look into the deepest parts of the universe."

"PAH!" snorted E-Dard Oo-Dard. "MOST VALRIK

BABIES CAN CONSTRUCT TELESCOPES CAPABLE OF SEEING TO THE ENDS OF THE UNIVERSE. AND YOUR SPACECRAFT ARE TERRIBLE. HOW FAR HAVE YOU GOT?"

"The spacecraft Voyager has travelled billions of miles," said Vinnie.

"PAH!" snorted E-Dard Oo-Dard again. "YOU'VE BARELY MADE IT OUT OF YOUR OWN SOLAR SYSTEM. IT'S PATHETIC. WE MIGHTY VALRIKIANS HAVE INVENTED A WAY TO TRAVEL FROM ONE END OF THE GALAXY TO THE OTHER. WHAT HAVE YOU DONE? YOU HAVE TRAVELLED TO YOUR MOON AND THEN SPENT THE REST OF YOUR TIME MAKING STICK-ON MOUSTACHES AND AUTOMATIC SWIMMING-TRUNK DRYERS

AND OUTFITS FOR DOGS. YOUR BRAINS ARE TINY AND PUNY."

E-Dard Oo-Dard stretched out his arm and poked Vinnie's shoulder with one of his talons. "WHAT MODS HAVE YOU GOT?"

"Mods?" said Eric.

"MODIFICATIONS," said E-Dard Oo-Dard.

"What do you mean?" said Vinnie.

E-Dard Oo-Dard popped out one of his eyeballs. "MY EYES CAN BE REMOVED AND USED AS REMOTE MICRO DRONES," he said, as his eyeball took off from his hand and flew around the room, before gliding back into its socket. "AND THAT'S NOT ALL, BECAUSE TREVOR HAS JUST HAD THE SPOONFINGER MOD INSTALLED."

Trevor smiled and held up his hands. His talons

retracted and were replaced by four different-sized spoons.

"VERY HANDY WHEN YOU'RE COOKING," said E-Dard Oo-Dard. "WHAT MODS HAVE YOU HAD?"

Eric looked at Vinnie and Vinnie looked at her shoes.

"Er, none," she said.

"NO MODIFICATIONS?" yelled E-Dard Oo-Dard.

"Disgusting!" screeched Trevor.

"Well, what about food then?" said Eric. "We can make some delicious food."

"AND WHICH DELICIOUS FOOD WOULD THIS BE?" scoffed E-Dard Oo-Dard. "THE COAGULATION OF SECRETIONS FROM LARGE FIELD-DWELLING MAMMALS THAT YOU LEAVE TO ROT FOR YEARS AND THEN PUT IN SANDWICHES OR ON TOAST."

"I think he means cheese," whispered Eric.

"OR PERHAPS YOU'RE REFERRING TO THE HARD OBJECTS THAT YOU EAT FOR BREAKFAST THAT COME OUT OF CHICKENS' BOTTOMS."

"Well, when you describe eggs like that, they do sound a bit odd," said Vinnie.

"IT'S NO WONDER THE PLANET UUURRTH

IS NAMED AFTER THE SOUND OF SOMEONE BEING SICK," said E-Dard Oo-Dard. "BECAUSE IT MUST HAPPEN A LOT."

He looked around the school hall, his red eyes scanning the room.

"AND SO WE COME TO THE LAST AREA FOR INSPECTION," he said. "THE HUMAN CHILDREN."

He turned and looked again into the live-streaming phone in Mr Flange's hand. "THEY REPRESENT THE FUTURE OF YOUR PLANET AND YET WE HAVEN'T SEEN A SINGLE CHILD WHO SEEMS TO KNOW HOW TO DO ANYTHING. WE HAVE WATCHED WHAT YOU SAID WERE THE FINEST TALENTS YOU HAD TO OFFER AND THEY WERE ALL AWFUL."

E-Dard Oo-Dard kept staring at the live-streaming phone. Tendrils of slobber dripped out of the sides of his mouth.

"IN SHORT, YOU HAVE FAILED AND SO WILL SHORTLY BE WIPED FROM THE FACE OF THE UNIVERSE. VAPORIZED IN AN INSTANT AND FORGOTTEN FOR ALL OF TIME."

Vinnie grabbed Eric's arm. "There's something we're missing," she whispered urgently. "Something that's not right."

But Eric wasn't listening, because he was looking out of the large windows at the back of the hall. Several police cars, ambulances and fire engines were squealing to a halt in the school car park.

"This is it," said Eric. "They've come to save us."

Eric watched as police officers tried to come in through the hall doors. But whatever E-Dard Oo-Dard had done to them had stuck them fast and they wouldn't budge. So next some fire officers brought out huge axes and began to try and chop the doors down. But no matter how hard they tried, their axes just seemed to bounce off. It was as if there was some kind of force field protecting the building. E-Dard Oo-Dard, who had been watching this activity with a sneer, held up his hands.

"ENOUGH!" he screeched.

And all the people on the outside of the school - the police officers, the paramedics, the fire fighters - they all just froze. It was like they were in a movie and someone had just pushed the pause button.

"HA!" said E-Dard Oo-Dard. "THAT SHOULD HOLD THEM."

A groan of disappointment filled the hall. Eric scanned the room, desperately searching for an escape route, one that might have been missed by the aliens. But there wasn't one. They were still stuck.

"RIGHT THEN," said E-Dard Oo-Dard. "LET'S GET THE VAPORIZING UNDER WAY. IT IS TIME TO ACT!"

A thought flashed through Vinnie's brain. "Of course!" she yelled. "Act! I knew there was something. You haven't seen Eric's act."

"What?" said Eric, who was now painfully aware that everyone was looking at him.

"ERIC?" said E-Dard Oo-Dard. "WHO IS THIS ERIC?"

Vinnie shoved Eric forward. Eric looked around.

"Er, hello," he said and gave a nervous little wave.

The live-streaming phone in Mr Flange's hand focused on him, broadcasting his face across the globe.

"You said you randomly pick a small area of the planet to inspect," said Vinnie.

"CORRECT!" said E-Dard Oo-Dard.

"Well, do you have to inspect all the children in that area?" said Vinnie.

E-Dard Oo-Dard looked at Trevor.

"No," said Trevor. "Section 210508 of the Intergalactic Convention states that we must inspect at least thirty of the life-form's young."

Vinnie jumped up and down. "Aha!" she said. "Well, you've only seen twenty-nine of us. Eric hasn't shown you his talent yet."

E-Dard Oo-Dard looked at Mrs Tittering.

"Er, she's right," said the head. "Eric was to perform last but he didn't get a chance."

E-Dard Oo-Dard prowled over to Trevor. "IS THIS A PROBLEM?"

"I'm afraid so, Your Mightiness," he said.

"Section 210508 is very clear about it."

"SO WE CAN'T JUST VAPORIZE THEM RIGHT NOW?"

"I'm afraid not, Your Mightiness," said Trevor.

E-Dard Oo-Dard turned back to the camera. "PEOPLE OF UUURRTHH, IT WOULD SEEM AS THOUGH YOU HAVE ONE LAST CHANCE," he said. "ONE FINAL OPPORTUNITY TO AVOID YOUR PLANET BEING DESTROYED. WE WILL SEE THIS 'ERIC', AND IF HE PERFORMS WELL AND GIVES US HOPE FOR THE FUTURE, THEN WE WILL SPARE YOUR SPECIES."

Vinnie gave Eric an encouraging look.

"HOWEVER," continued E-Dard Oo-Dard, "IF HE PERFORMS BADLY, WHICH I'M SURE HE WILL, THEN WE WILL VAPORIZE YOU ALL."

"Wait!" said Eric. "Are you saying that the continuation of humans as a species is entirely dependent on my act in the talent show?"

"YES!" bellowed E-Dard Oo-Dard.

Vinnie turned to Eric.

"No pressure then," she said. "Good luck."

THE VANISHING ACT OF THE MYSTICAL MOUSE OF MYSTERY

Eric Doomsday might have been Earth's last hope, but he didn't feel like it. No, as he stood at the back of the stage in a pair of silver sequinned trousers, a tight green sparkly off-the-shoulder top, and a purple baseball cap that had Mr Awesome written on the front, Eric felt like

the last wazzock in the shop.

"I raided my mum's wardrobe for most of it," said Vinnie. "But the hat is my Uncle Bert's."

"I look stupid," said Eric.

"You do not," said Vinnie. "You look very, er, mysterious. I bet Barry Cheeseballs would wear it."

"I bet he wouldn't," said Eric.

"Well, don't worry about it now," said Vinnie. "Have you got everything?"

Eric looked under his chair. He had carefully packed everything into a cardboard box. The beautiful silk scarves for the first trick, the deck of cards for the trick with Mr Magique, the jug and glass for the last trick and the smoke bombs for his Big Spectacular Exit.

"WE'RE WAITING!" screeched E-Dard Oo-Dard from the front of the stage.

Eric looked at all his Year Six classmates, who were still sitting on the bench at the back of stage. Some were crying, some were hugging each other in fear, others were simply staring dead ahead, their brains not quite believing what was going on around them.

"So," he said. "It's all down to me then."

Vinnie adjusted his cap. "Don't think about it," she said. "Just imagine how popular you're going to be if you can pull this off. You'll be more popular than Hattie, Grace and Drishya put together. And if not, well, we'll all be dead. Now, is everything ready?"

Eric nodded. "I think so," he said, grabbing the three smoke bombs from the box and putting them in his pocket. "I just need to set up the trick with Mr Magique."

Grabbing his deck of cards, Eric removed the sparkly cloth from Mr Magique's cage - and discovered that it was empty. The small door on the side of the cage was open and Mr Magique was nowhere to be seen.

"Where is he?" he hissed.

Vinnie looked at the empty cage and then dropped to the floor. "Mr Magique? Here, boy. Where are you?" she called, over and over. "He's always doing this. Come on, boy, where are you?"

"What do you mean, 'he's always doing this'?" said Eric, rubbing his temples. "He can't do this now. I need him."

"WE'RE STILL WAITING!" screamed E-Dard Oo-Dard.

Despite a frantic search, Mr Magique could not be found anywhere.

"Don't worry," said Vinnie. "I'm sure he'll turn up."

"What am I going to do about the trick?" said Eric, pacing around the back of the stage.

"Don't worry," said Vinnie. "Just do the first trick. I'll keep looking and if I find him I'll bring him on for you."

"What if you don't find him?"

"Then just finish with the trick you showed me and use the smoke bombs," said Vinnie. "It'll all be fine."

Mrs Tittering came over to them. "It's now or never," she said. "Good luck."

"Good luck, Eric," said Vinnie. "You'll be amazing."

"Good luck, Eric," said Lenny Frisby.

"Good luck, Eric," said Lizzie Worney.

"Good luck, Eric," said Elton Gweek.

"Good luck, Eric," said Drishya Samode.

"Good luck, Eric," said Luis Agueda.

"Good luck, Eric," said Tom Boosbeck.

"Good luck, Eric," said the kid-whose-name-no-one-could-quite-remember.

"Er, thanks, er, Barry?" said Eric, desperately trying to think of his name.

"It's Ian," said Ian, and he went and sat down.

One by one, each of Eric's Year Six classmates came up to him and wished him good luck. Even Hattie Lavernock.

"Good luck, Eric," she said and gave him a hug.

"Er, thanks," said Eric, flushing bright red and not knowing where to look. His only previous hugs from any females had been from his mum and his two grandmas. He was not comfortable with it at all.

A hush fell across the school hall as Mrs Tittering slowly walked to the front of the stage. Every squeak of her shoes echoed around the room. Finally, she took her position and looked out at the terrified faces of the pupils and teachers. She paused and took a deep breath. "And now," she said, trying to find a reassuring smile, "it is time for our final act. The one, the only, Eric Doomsday."

Eric walked to the front of the stage and looked out at the audience sitting in the hall. Some were sobbing, some were frowning, all looked scared. But on each and every one of their faces, Eric saw something else too. It was hope. They were all watching and waiting and hoping that a boy in slightly-too-big silver sequinned trousers, a tight green sparkly off-the-shoulder top, and a purple baseball cap that had *Mr Awesome* written on the front, would be able to save the world.

THE EARTH'S LAST HOPE

Eric's first trick went well – really well. In fact, it went better than he could ever have dared hope. He performed the silk scarves trick perfectly.

"No way!" screamed Trevor, when Eric tucked the last scarf into his fist, then unfurled his fingers to reveal his empty hand. "How did you do that?"

"HMMMMM," said E-Dard Oo-Dard. "IMPRESSIVE."

With the first trick over, Eric looked at Vinnie.

She held up an empty cage and shook her head. Without Mr Magique, Eric had to move straight on to the gravity-defying water-in-the-glass trick that he'd shown Vinnie the day before. Although, with one slight adjustment.

"For my next trick," he announced, "I will need a volunteer. Would anyone like to come up onstage?"

Eric had decided to take Vinnie's advice and was going to hold the upside-down glass of water over someone's head for extra dramatic impact. He scanned the room for a potential volunteer, but all he could see was hundreds of terrified faces staring at the two huge aliens with their elongated skulls and horrible red eyes. Eric heard a grunting noise coming from the judges' table. He turned and saw Trevor was holding his long sinewy arms in the air as high as they could go.

"Me, me, me, me, me, me," he grunted. "Pick me. I'll be your volunteer."

"Er, okay," said Eric, pointing at Trevor. "Let's have a big round of applause for our volunteer."

Hardly anyone clapped. To be fair though, the sight of a three-metre-tall alien bounding across the stage and doing what looked like jazz hands with his hideous claws was a little distressing.

Eric guided Trevor to the middle of the stage and sat him down on a chair. The chair groaned and buckled under his weight. Eric grabbed the glass from his cardboard box of props.

"Behold the Glass of Emptiness," said Eric, holding the empty glass up for the audience to see. He put the glass down on a small table in front of him and reached into his cardboard box again.

"Now observe the Jug of Hideousness," he said, pulling out a jug full of green liquid. He took the jug over to the judges to let them see it. E-Dard Oo-Dard tapped it suspiciously.

"WHAT'S THAT?" he said. "WHY IS IT GREEN?"

199

"Er, it's just water really," whispered Eric. "With a bit of food dye in it."

Actually, in an effort to make the green water look even more magical, Eric had taken Vinnie's advice and also tipped a whole box of hundreds and thousands in. They'd looked great to begin with – all colourful and sparkly – but then they'd dissolved. He didn't bother to mention his sparkle failure. Instead, he dipped his finger into the jug and licked it.

"See?" He smiled. "It's harmless."

"HMMM," said E-Dard Oo-Dard. "ALRIGHT THEN, GET ON WITH IT."

Eric had no way of knowing it, but while dissolved hundreds and thousands were harmless to humans, they were not harmless to E-Dard Oo-Dard and Trevor. Not at all. In fact, sugar was deadly poisonous to aliens from the planet Valrik.

Eric poured some of the green water into the glass and set the jug down on the judging table. Then he walked slowly back to where Trevor was sitting, the audience watching his every move. Eric saw the red light blink on Mr Flange's phone as it streamed his trick to the world.

"I will now use my magic powers to defy the laws of gravity," he said, placing his special piece of cardboard over the top of the glass and turning the whole thing upside down. The hall was completely silent. No one dared move, no one even dared breathe. They were all desperately willing Eric to successfully complete his trick.

Eric removed his hand from the piece of card, which stayed in place and stopped the green liquid from falling out.

"THAT'S PATHETIC!" shouted E-Dard Oo-Dard. "IT'S OBVIOUSLY BEING HELD UP BY SUCTION. THAT'S NOT IN THE SLIGHTEST BIT MAGICAL OR GOOD."

A nervous murmur fluttered around the hall. But Eric wasn't finished. He held the upside-down glass above Trevor's head. The alien's brain twitched and bulged beneath the papery thin skin on the top of his head.

Eric took one last calming breath and concentrated like he had never concentrated before.

"Behold my magic powers," he said, and quickly pulled the cardboard away from under the glass.

The audience gasped, expecting the disgusting green liquid to fall over Trevor's head... But it stayed in the glass.

It took a moment for everyone in the hall to realize that the trick had worked – but when they did, the whole school burst into applause. Eric stood there, still holding the upside-down glass over Trevor's head, as relief and excitement erupted in the school hall. He saw Mrs Tittering leap to her feet, yelling and clapping her hands. Next to her, Ms Lotte from the council was cheering. Everyone in the audience was applauding and stamping their feet and chanting his name: "ER-IC, ER-IC, ER-IC." Even E-Dard

Oo-Dard and Trevor were applauding.

He had done it. He had performed a magic routine where nothing had gone wrong! He turned and saw Vinnie rushing over to him and all of his Year Six classmates cheering and whooping. Could it be that he had saved the world from being vaporized AND become the most popular person in the school? And he hadn't even used his smoke bombs!

It was then, just as he was thinking that this might be the best day ever, that Eric saw something moving out of the corner of his eye. Something fast. Something fast and hamster-like. Something fast and hamster-like that was racing towards the judges' table.

THE AMAZING (BUT BADLY-TIMED) REAPPEARANCE OF THE MYSTICAL MOUSE OF MYSTERY

"W-W-W-WHAT'S THAT?" shrieked E-Dard Oo-Dard as he watched Mr Magique zip across the stage and dart up his long, sinewy leg. He leaped up and began hopping around.

"It's just Mr Magique!" shouted Eric. "He's only a hamster."

"He won't hurt you," said Vinnie.

But E-Dard Oo-Dard wasn't listening, because Mr Magique's little scampery legs and twitching

206

nose absolutely terrified him. He stumbled backwards and fell off the stage into a row of screaming reception pupils. As he fell, his foot caught the underside of the judges' table and flipped it over. Everything on the table got thrown up into the air – the pens for making notes, the scoring paddles, Mrs Tittering's best biscuits and the jug filled with water and green food dye and dissolved hundreds and thousands all flew across the stage.

Eric was just thinking how much this reminded him of Hattie Lavernock's birthday party when the jug spun and flipped right past him and showered green sugary water all over Trevor.

The moment the mixture came into contact with the alien's see-through head and glistening, muscular body, its horrific effect took hold. Because there wasn't any sugar on the planet Valrik, their bodies were simply unable to cope when they came into contact with it. Trevor let out a scream the like of which had never been heard before on Earth. It was a cry of pain and a plea for help all wrapped up in one hideous noise that only lasted for a moment but seemed to go on for eternity.

"TREVOR!" yelled E-Dard Oo-Dard, scrambling back onto the stage.

Trevor looked over at E-Dard Oo-Dard, then shuddered a little...and then exploded. Just like that.

The school hall and all the Dreary Inkling pupils were splattered in slobber and gunk and slime. It went everywhere. All over their hair and in their eyes and up their noses and in their mouths and all over their arms and bodies and legs and hands. Eric stood on the stage and wiped the exploded alien gunk off his face. E-Dard Oo-Dard prowled towards him.

"YOU'VE KILLED TREVOR," he hissed. "THIS IS AN ACT OF WAR. YOUR PATHETIC PLANET WILL BE VAPORIZED FOR THIS."

The next thing anyone in the Dreary Inkling Primary School hall saw was a bright, white flash of light – and when it was over, Eric, Vinnie and E-Dard Oo-Dard had vanished.

THE LAST ROOM YOU'LL EVER SEE

Eric blinked and rubbed his eyes. He had a sicky, dizzy feeling deep in his stomach, just like that time three years ago when he'd accidentally put a slug in his mouth because he thought it was a cocktail sausage that had fallen on the floor. He blinked a bit more and, slowly, as his eyes adjusted, the whiteness began to fade. Eric could now see that he was standing on a large red circle in the middle of a dimly-lit room. Multicoloured lights flashed and winked at him from the wall opposite. It looked like some sort of control panel. There was a large dial, right in the middle of the blinking lights, with a big red button next to it.

"Ohhhhhhhhhhhhhh."

He heard a soft moaning from beside him. It was Vinnie.

"You okay?" he whispered.

Vinnie nodded, although it wasn't a very convincing nod. It was more like the kind of nod you give when you want someone to think you're alright but the truth is that you have never been more scared in your whole life. Eric gave her a reassuring smile and, even though it went against all his previous eleven-year training on how to deal with girls, he grabbed her hand and gave it a quick squeeze. It was the kind of thing that his mum did when he felt frightened and it usually did the trick.

"DISGUSTING HUMANS," boomed a horrible but familiar voice from behind them. Eric turned and saw E-Dard Oo-Dard standing there, his red eyes burning in the gloom. "YOU ARE NOW IN THE TELEPORTATION CHAMBER ON BOARD THE GALAXY INSPECTORS' SPACECRUISER 689908. FROM HERE WE WILL MOVE TO THE FLIGHT DECK, WHERE YOU WILL HAVE A PERFECT VIEW OF THE DESTRUCTION OF YOUR PLANET BEFORE YOU ARE BOTH BLASTED TO YOUR DEATHS IN THE DEPTHS OF SPACE."

Eric thought about asking why they didn't

have a teleportation chamber on the flight deck, but decided now probably wasn't quite the right time. A door swooshed open in front of them.

"MOVE!" screamed E-Dard Oo-Dard.

Outside the teleportation chamber was a long corridor, with an enormous floor-to-ceiling window along one side. Eric gasped as he looked out and saw, far below them, the whole of the planet Earth. From high up in space, it seemed so small. Eric couldn't believe that down there were not only his mum and dad and grandma and grandpa and aunts and uncles and cousins, but all the other millions of mums and dads and grandmas and grandpas and aunts and uncles and cousins too. He didn't know how they all fitted in. As he walked, he stared at the Earth, unable to look away. He thought about all the people who were living there now and everyone who had ever lived on that small ball of rock. All the kings and queens and teachers and farmers and prime ministers and presidents and hunters and gatherers and pharaohs and emperors and soldiers and cave dwellers and blue whales and butterflies and dinosaurs.

"Look at that," said Vinnie, as wisps of white cloud moved silently across vast oceans of blue. "It's so beautiful."

And Eric had to agree that it was.

"SILENCE!" screeched E-Dard Oo-Dard. "YOUR PLANET IS HIDEOUS AND REVOLTING AND NOT AT ALL BEAUTIFUL."

At the end of the corridor, E-Dard Oo-Dard

stopped outside a closed door. He placed a talon inside a small hole in the wall and the door swooshed open. Eric and Vinnie walked through and found themselves in an enormous room. There were huge banks of computer screens at the back but the rest of the room was all glass. To his left, Eric could still see the Earth, but straight ahead was the moon, bigger than he had ever seen it before, set against the vast darkness of the universe.

"WELCOME TO THE FLIGHT DECK," said E-Dard Oo-Dard. "IT IS THE LAST ROOM YOU WILL EVER SEE."

THE PLANET-VAPORIZING RAY

Eric felt his stomach sinking through the floor as he stood next to Vinnie on the flight deck.

"THIS IS THE NERVE CENTRE OF OUR SPACECRUISER," said E-Dard Oo-Dard. "EVERYTHING IS CONTROLLED FROM IN HERE. I CAN FLY THE SPACECRUISER FROM IN HERE, I CAN TOP UP THE DRINKS DISPENSER ON LEVEL THREE FROM IN HERE, AND I CAN USE OUR FULLY

OPERATIONAL, 360-DEGREE, TITANIUM-AND-LEATHER VAPORIZING RAY TO DESTROY PLANETS FROM IN HERE."

Eric watched as E-Dard Oo-Dard's long, forked tongue flickered over his razor-sharp teeth. He felt his stomach sink a little further through the floor.

"PERHAPS YOU'D LIKE TO MOVE A LITTLE CLOSER AND SEE THE CONTROL PANEL OF THE PLANET-VAPORIZING RAY," he said. "IT IS A WEAPON SO POWERFUL THAT IT CAN BLOW UP A PLANET IN A MATTER OF SECONDS. AND SOON IT WILL."

E-Dard Oo-Dard pointed at a large bank of winking lights and pushed a couple of buttons.

Eric and Vinnie shuffled forward and looked out of the giant window. Outside, an enormous telescopic arm extended from the side of the ship. E-Dard Oo-Dard pushed another button on the control panel and a huge silver nozzle with leather racing trim unfolded from the end of the arm. Eric gulped and looked at Vinnie.

"BEHOLD THE PLANET-VAPORIZING RAY!" said E-Dard Oo-Dard.

Eric was about to speak when his hand brushed against his trouser pocket and he felt something. Something he had quite forgotten about. Well, three somethings he had quite forgotten about, actually.

"That's incredible," he heard Vinnie say. "How does it work?"

Eric put his hand in his pocket and ran his fingers over the three small, round objects. An idea began to stir deep inside his brain.

"PAH," slobbered E-Dard Oo-Dard. "I COULD TELL YOU HOW THE PLANET-VAPORIZING RAY WORKS BUT YOUR SPECIES IS TOO STUPID TO UNDERSTAND."

Vinnie looked at the control panel. There was a series of dials and switches and one big red button. "Is it some sort of particle beam?" she said.

E-Dard Oo-Dard narrowed his eyes. "ERM, YES, IT IS SOME SORT OF PARTICLE BEAM, BUT THAT MUST HAVE BEEN A LUCKY GUESS. WHAT YOUR PUNY BRAIN DOESN'T UNDERSTAND IS THAT IT IS A VERY SPECIFIC TYPE OF PARTICLE BEAM."

Vinnie gave the control panel another once-over. "It's not gamma particles, I don't think," she said. "It looks to me like some kind of plasma ray."

"WELL, YES, THAT'S CORRECT AS WELL!" said E-Dard Oo-Dard. "WHICH MUST HAVE BEEN ANOTHER LUCKY GUESS. BUT IT DOES NOT MATTER THAT YOU KNOW WHAT SPECIFIC TYPE OF RAY IT IS, BECAUSE YOUR WEAK AND FEEBLE MINDS WOULD NEVER UNDERSTAND HOW TO USE IT."

E-Dard Oo-Dard began twiddling a dial that was just like the one Eric had noticed in the teleportation room. The numbers 290-519-68 appeared on a screen.

"What are those numbers?" he asked.

E-Dard Oo-Dard looked at him and snarled.

"NONE OF YOUR BUSINESS," he snapped.

"They must be co-ordinates of some sort," said Vinnie. "Probably of the thing you want the ray to blow up. So, I'm guessing they must be the co-ordinates of Earth?"

E-Dard Oo-Dard didn't say anything, he just turned back to the control panel and twiddled another dial. The numbers 000-000-00 appeared on a different screen.

"And if those first numbers are the co-ordinates of Earth, then those must be the co-ordinates of the ship, because the ray would need to know where it is firing from and where it is firing to." Vinnie pointed at a large red button in the middle of the control panel. "And I guess that must be the firing button."

"SILENCE!" said E-Dard Oo-Dard. "IT DOES NOT MATTER THAT YOU KNOW WHAT TYPE OF SPECIFIC RAY WE HAVE AND EXACTLY HOW TO WORK IT, BECAUSE ALL THAT MATTERS IS THAT YOU ARE GOING TO PUSH THE BUTTON ON THE PLANET-VAPORIZING RAY AND VAPORIZE YOUR OWN DISGUSTING PLANET, AS A PUNISHMENT FOR KILLING TREVOR."

"What?" said Eric. "But that was an accident! And how were we supposed to know that the Jug of Hideousness could kill Trevor? Maybe you're allergic to water. My gran is allergic to cheese, she comes out in a really bad rash if she goes anywhere near so much as a cheese slice." He thought for a moment. "Although she hasn't ever exploded," he added.

"SILENCE!" yelled E-Dard Oo-Dard. "OF COURSE WE'RE NOT ALLERGIC TO WATER. THE SURFACE OF YOUR PATHETIC PLANET IS EIGHTY PER CENT WATER. WE WOULDN'T HAVE COME IF WE WERE ALLERGIC TO WATER, WOULD WE? NO, YOU CLEARLY POISONED THE LIQUID ON PURPOSE TO DESTROY US." His tongue flicked around his lips. "BUT NOW YOU ARE THE ONES WHO WILL BE DESTROYED."

E-Dard Oo-Dard turned back to the control panel and began twiddling some more dials. "RIGHT, AFTER YOU HAVE PUSHED THE FIRING BUTTON THERE IS A TWENTY-SECOND DELAY WHILE THE PLASMA

CREATES A LARGE ENOUGH CHARGE TO DESTROY YOUR PLANET."

While E-Dard Oo-Dard's back was turned, Eric grabbed Vinnie's hand. This took her by surprise, but she went against all her previous eleven-year training on how to deal with boys and let him – it was the end of the world, after all. But Eric didn't want to hold her hand, he wanted to give her something.

"Can it be stopped?" he said, trying to speak as casually as he could. "Once we've pushed the button, I mean?"

E-Dard Oo-Dard shook his enormous, elongated head. Eric, standing behind him, could again see the alien's brain pulsing and quivering.

"ABSOLUTELY NOT," said E-Dard Oo-Dard.

"ONCE THE BUTTON IS PUSHED, THE PLANET IS DOOMED."

Vinnie glanced down at her hand and saw that Eric had given her a small, round smoke bomb. She looked at him. He held up a smoke bomb in his hand too. He pointed at her, then at the smoke bombs, then at a bank of computers at the back of the room. Vinnie nodded, understanding immediately what they were about to do. She gave Eric their special secret smile where she curled her fingers around her top lip like a moustache (though still hiding the smoke bomb) and opened her eyes as wide as they would go, and Eric did it back.

"In three, two, one..." Eric mouthed – then he and Vinnie lobbed their smoke bombs at the

computers, where they silently exploded, throwing up two great plumes of smoke.

E-Dard Oo-Dard sniffed the air.

"WAIT, WHAT'S THAT SMELL?" he said and turned around from the control panel.

"Er, I think your flight deck is on fire," said Eric, pointing at the smoke that was now billowing out from behind the computers.

"PUT IT OUT!" screamed E-Dard Oo-Dard, rushing over to the smoke. "PUT IT OUT!"

But as he screeched and jumped and wafted his arms around as fast as he could, E-Dard Oo-Dard didn't notice the next bit of Eric's plan being put into effect.

THE BIG
SPECTACULAR EXIT

After a minute of furious arm-wafting, E-Dard Oo-Dard glanced back over at Eric and Vinnie. Through the smoke, he thought he could see them twiddling the dials on the planet-vaporizing ray's control panel.

"WHAT ARE YOU DOING?" he screamed.

Eric turned around, his finger hovering over the red firing button. "Do you want to know what caused the smoke?" he said.

"WHAT?" said E-Dard Oo-Dard, still wafting his arms.

"We did," said Eric, holding up the last smoke bomb. "With these."

A look of confusion spread across E-Dard Oo-Dard's face. Or, at least, Eric thought it was a look of confusion. With three-metre-tall aliens with papery skin and large snarling mouths, it can sometimes be tricky to tell.

"We needed you out of the way, so we caused a little distraction," said Vinnie.

"Magicians call it misdirection," said Eric.

"WHAT DO YOU MEAN, YOU NEEDED ME OUT OF THE WAY? WHAT FOR?" snapped E-Dard Oo-Dard, who began prowling back towards the control panel.

"So we could do this!" Eric said, and hit the big red firing button.

"PLANET-VAPORIZING RAY ACTIVATED!" blared a loud mechanical voice from the control panel. "TWENTY SECONDS UNTIL BLASTING!"

Eric turned and threw the smoke bomb onto the floor in front of them. "Come on, let's go!"

Under the cover of the third huge plume of smoke, Eric and Vinnie raced back across the flight deck and out through the door.

E-Dard Oo-Dard scrambled and spluttered and coughed his way back to the planet-vaporizing ray's control panel, where a thought occurred to him. What if someone had used the recent smoke-induced chaos to change the co-ordinates that the ray was going to fire at? Just after he had that thought, E-Dard Oo-Dard checked to see if the planet-vaporizing ray was still set to blast the Earth. Just after *that*, E-Dard Oo-Dard realized that it wasn't and that the ray had in fact now been set to blast the Galaxy Inspectors' SpaceCruiser.

That was Eric and Vinnie's plan. They were going to blow up the ship.

"*FIFTEEN SECONDS UNTIL BLASTING!*" blared the loud mechanical voice from the control panel.

"STOP!" screeched E-Dard Oo-Dard, as he bounded for the door.

In the teleportation chamber, Eric looked at the bank of computers and saw a dial and a big red firing button that looked just like the ones on the planet-vaporizing ray's control panel.

"Quick, Vinnie," he shouted. "Get on the red circle."

"*TEN SECONDS UNTIL BLASTING!*" blared the loud mechanical voice.

Eric looked back down the corridor and saw E-Dard Oo-Dard leaping through the flight deck door and heading towards them. He turned the dial until the numbers 290-519-68 appeared. The co-ordinates for Earth.

"What about you?" yelled Vinnie, as she raced onto the red platform.

"I'm coming too," he roared and hit the big red button.

"*FIVE SECONDS UNTIL BLASTING!*"

Eric ran towards the platform. The circle changed colour from red to yellow.

"*FOUR!*"

Vinnie suddenly started to glow – she was about to teleport.

"*THREE!*"

Eric was still running towards Vinnie when E-Dard Oo-Dard rushed through the teleportation chamber door.

"*TWO!*"

The circle changed from yellow to green.

"I'M NOT GOING TO MAKE IT!" screamed Eric.

"TAKE MY HAND!" shouted Vinnie and she reached out as far as she could.

But as he raced towards her, Eric tripped over some wires on the floor and stumbled.

"ERIC!" screamed Vinnie.

E-Dard Oo-Dard leaped towards Eric, trying to grab onto him – but as he did, Eric's stumble turned into a full-on plunge through the air and his flailing left foot somehow booted E-Dard Oo-Dard right in the face.

"ONE!"

There was a huge, white, blinding FLASH!

And everything went dark.

Eric opened his eyes and saw that he was lying on the floor of the school stage. Vinnie's face beamed next to him. He looked down by his side and saw that, despite all his previous eleven-year training on how to deal with girls, he was clutching his best friend's hand like his life depended on it.

Which, of course, it had.

By the time he'd pulled himself upright and taken a moment to get over the shock of not being vaporized, official confirmation from NASA and the other world space agencies was being broadcast across the planet: the Galaxy Inspectors' SpaceCruiser 689908 had been destroyed and the Earth was safe.

Eric and Vinnie stood on the stage and filled everyone in on exactly what had happened inside the ship. Once they had finished, Mrs Tittering held their arms aloft in triumph and everyone burst into wild applause. Soon, people from outside began pouring into the school hall, all cheering and applauding too.

"We did it, Eric," said Vinnie. "We only went and did it." She gave Eric another of their special secret smiles.

"What's our popularity number now?" said Eric, as he and Vinnie listened to hundreds of people chanting their names.

Vinnie turned and watched as Steve Enjoy scampered out from the side of the stage and up Mr Flange's left trouser leg. Mr Flange, who obviously wasn't used to things scampering up his left trouser leg, leaped backwards in shock and fell off the stage into a group of Year Ones.

"We are off the chart, Eric Doomsday," said Vinnie. "We are off the flippin' chart."

THURSDAY

From: Lotte, Priscilla <lotte.priscilla@thecouncil>

CC: <ramsbottom.ivor@thecouncil>; <doodoo.

ivana@thecouncil>

To: Tittering, Elvira <headteacher@

drearyschool1>

Dear Mrs Tittering,

After an emergency late-night meeting of the

education department, I am writing to inform

you that, following recent global events, the

council has decided it will NOT be closing down

your school after all. I have chatted with my

colleagues, who I have included in this email,

and we believe that any school that produces

pupils as brave and resourceful as Eric

Doomsday and Vinnie Mumbles must be doing something right.

We have also sent you a cheque for £100,000 to spend on equipment and books and to fill in the holes in the playground. We are so proud of everything you have achieved in the last week.

Yours sincerely,

Ms P.A. Lotte

Mr Ivor Ramsbottom

Ms Ivana Doo-Doo

243

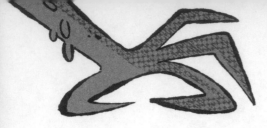

FRIDAY

BARRY CHEESEBALLS

"Hi, guys," said Barry Cheeseballs with a cheesy grin. "And welcome to a very special video with some very special guests."

Since saving the world from alien destruction, Eric and Vinnie had received thousands of interview requests from TV stations all over the planet, but they only wanted to do one. Eric had nearly fainted when he'd heard that his favourite internet sensation, Barry Cheeseballs, wanted him on his YouTube channel. And so here they were, sitting on Barry's Throne of Magic inside his Palace of Wonder. Although it had come as a bit of a disappointment to Eric to find out that the Throne of Magic was actually a single bed covered with a sparkly cloth and the Palace of Wonder was just Barry's mum's spare bedroom.

"So, Eric Doomsday and Vinnie Mumbles," said Barry Cheeseballs, talking into a camera he had set up on the window sill. "It's great to have you in the Palace of Wonder. How does it feel to be the most famous people in the world?"

Eric paused. He was sort of hypnotized by the strange smell in the Palace of Wonder. It was like a mixture of sweaty feet and tinned fish. "It's been a bit weird," he said.

"Yeah," said Vinnie. "We've already spoken to thirty-four different world leaders since Wednesday."

Eric nodded. "But really we just want things to get back to normal," he said. "We just want to be treated like regular kids again and not like unbelievably heroic and amazing saviours of the entire human race."

Barry Cheeseballs turned to the camera and flashed a wide smile. "Can you believe it, Cheesers?" he said (he always referred to anyone who watched his channel as a Cheeser). "They've just saved the world from being destroyed and all they want is for things to get back to normal. Incredible."

Eric noticed a bit of spinach stuck between Barry Cheeseballs's teeth.

"Well, we've got a surprise for you two," said Barry. "The whole world was super-impressed by what you did, but one very special person wanted to say hello."

Eric heard the door of Barry's mum's spare room open. He and Vinnie turned around in shock to see Barry's mum show in the Prime Minister.

"Prime Minister," said Barry Cheeseballs. "Welcome to the Palace of Wonder."

"Thanks, Barry," said the Prime Minister, sitting

down on the end of the Throne of Magic. "I'm a total Cheeser. I watch your channel all the time."

"Really?" said Vinnie. "I'd have thought you had much more important things to do."

The Prime Minister smiled. "You're right," he said. "There's a lot of *Animals Doing the Funniest*

Things Wearing People's Underwear to get through, isn't there?"

Eric looked at Vinnie and rolled his eyes.

"So, Prime Minister," said Barry Cheeseballs. "I know you have something to say to Eric and Vinnie."

The Prime Minister gave a little cough. "Yes, Barry, thank you," he said, staring at the camera. "First of all, I want to make absolutely clear that even though Eric and Vinnie sorted things out and saved the planet, I had just come up with a brilliant plan to get rid of the aliens myself and was about to put it into action when Eric and Vinnie blew up the Galaxy Inspectors' ship."

"Oh really?" said Eric suspiciously. "What was the plan?"

The Prime Minister paused for a moment and

Eric thought he saw the tiniest bead of sweat trickle down the side of his face. "Oh, we don't need to worry about that now," he said with a bit of a wobble in his voice. "Today is not about me and how brilliant at Prime Ministering I am. Today is about you two."

The Prime Minister smiled and turned to Barry Cheeseballs. "Do you know, Barry, I didn't think anything could top last year's final of *Britain's Bott Talent*. But Eric Doomsday and Vinnie Mumbles destroying those aliens was even more impressive than when Doris Buttermere attempted to fart the Lithuanian national anthem underwater. I am recommending that they be given knighthoods in a special ceremony after we've finished here."

Barry Cheeseballs gasped.

"This will mean," continued the Prime Minister, "that Eric will be the youngest ever knight and Vinnie the first female knight in the history of the country."

"That is amazing, Prime Minister," said Barry Cheeseballs. "But before that special ceremony begins, and in celebration of Eric's terrific performance in front of the aliens, I think we should ask him to do some magic for us. Don't you agree?"

"Oh yes," said the Prime Minister, clapping his hands together in delight. "That's a terrific idea."

Eric shifted nervously in his seat.

"How about it, Eric?" said Barry Cheeseballs.

Eric looked at Vinnie. She smiled at him and nodded.

"Go on," she said, and she gave him their special secret smile where she curled her fingers around her top lip like a moustache and opened her eyes as wide as they would go.

Actually, now Eric thought about it, there was a trick he could do. One that he hadn't shown anyone before. If he got it right, he just knew that everyone would love it.

"Come on, Eric," said Barry Cheeseballs. "I mean, what can possibly go wrong?"

Barry Cheeseballs didn't know it, but he was about to regret those ill-chosen words. You see, between the pressure of being live on the internet, the Prime Minister sitting next to him, and the fact that he could see a pair of underpants sitting on a dirty plate by Barry Cheeseballs's feet, Eric's magic trick did NOT go according to plan. In fact, it went so badly, and what Eric accidentally did to the Prime Minister was so awful, that it was decided by Eric, Vinnie, Barry Cheeseballs, Barry Cheeseballs's mum, the police, the local council, the European Court for Human Rights, and all the millions of people watching online that they would never, ever, EVER speak of what happened in Barry Cheeseballs's mum's spare bedroom ever again.

Acknowledgements

My first big THANK YOU has to go to my son Sam. Not only was he the first person who read the finished story, he also came up with the three best names in the book: Barry Cheeseballs, Johnny Smuthers and the brilliantly named Steve Enjoy. Thanks too, to all my AWESOME family, especially Liz and Joe, who put up with me when I'm writing and I can't concentrate on anything else.

Massive thanks, as ever, to team Usborne who are all AMAZING and BRILLIANT, but super-special mentions (and secret smiles) to Rebecca, Sarah S, Will, Sarah C, Liz, Hannah and Stevie.

Great whopping thanks to Non Pratt and Robin Stevens who showed me that my second sentence would, in fact, make a better first sentence. They were so right.

Huge thanks to Paco for bringing Dreary Inkling to life with his genius illustrations (especially Eric's off-the-shoulder sparkly top!).

Thanks to YouTubers Mismag822 and EvanEraTV (for the magic tutorials), Martin Gardner (I got the number trick on page 86 from his book *Mathematics, Magic & Mystery*), Carl Sagan and his Pale Blue Dot, Richard and Sir Adrian Dangerous, Abbot & Costello, the Adam & Joe Radio Show (where I first heard a joke about a disobedient dog called Minton), Ross Beresford (who told me about Valrik), and to the person who told me the joke, "Why does Edward Woodward have so many w's in his name? Because otherwise he'd be Edard Oodard!". To any aliens reading this I'd like to say BLJJGJHFHKDRF HHFDHFCHC HMGCHGFH FGHFGKHGFK GKGNVB (they'll understand).

Finally, a humongous THANKS to Becky Walker and Jenny Savill, without whom this book would not have been written. They guided, cajoled, helped, soothed and inspired me all the way. Thank you both from the bottom of my heart.